"Hare," watercolor by Albrecht Dürer

The
7th
Knot

The 7th Knot

by

Kathleen

Karr

Marshall Cavendish

New York

Cavendish Children's Books
Marshall Cavendish
99 White Plains Road
Tarrytown, New York 10591
www.marshallcavendish.com

Albrecht Dürer's "Hare," copyright © Erich Lessing / Art Resource, NY
Albrecht Dürer's "Self-portrait with Sea Holly," copyright © Reunion
des Musees Nationaux / Art Resource, NY

Library of Congress Cataloging-in-Publication Data
Karr, Kathleen.
The seventh knot / by Kathleen Karr.
p. cm.
Summary: Two brothers touring Europe in the 19th century become
embroiled in a mystery involving Albrecht Dürer's knot woodcuts and a
secret German society when they go in search of their uncle's enigmatic
missing valet.
ISBN 0-7614-5135-8
[1. Brothers--Fiction. 2. Dürer, Albrecht, 1471-1528--Fiction. 3.
Art--Fiction. 4. Mystery and detective stories.] I. Title.
PZ7.K149 Se 2003
[Fic]--dc21
2002015547

The text of this book is set in 11-point Goudy Old Style.
Book design by Anahid Hamparian

The designs in each chapter opening are reproductions of four knots from
Albrecht Dürer's "Knot" series of woodcuts.

Printed in the United States of America
3 5 6 4 2

For Daniel, at last!

The
7th
Knot

One

"But it was only a *little* bomb, Mother."

Miles Forrester's chin jutted toward his glowering parent. "It wouldn't have hurt my Latin master."

"Much," offered Wick, Miles's spectacularly unhelpful older brother.

Mrs. Forrester was unconvinced. "I'm certain your Latin master does not share that opinion."

Wick snickered.

"Chadwick Hoving Forrester the Third, I'm speaking to you too. You *both* had disastrous school reports. Stand up straight!"

"Yes, Mother." Wick sighed and shifted the weight of his lanky frame from one leg to the other. Mrs. Forrester eyed her elder son with distaste.

"You do realize it was only through your parents' intervention that you were allowed to finish your school term?" Her tone was more lethal than acid. "Rather than being ignominiously expelled?"

"Yes, Mother." Wick shifted again.

"Have you nothing further to say, young man?"

Wick halfheartedly covered a yawn. "School is all such a bore. I don't see the harm in trotting off for a cigar once in a while."

"You don't see the harm in leaving your boarding school without permission? In smoking a cigar at the age of fifteen? In contributing to the delinquency of your friends by coercing them into joining you?"

That got a rise out of Wick. "On the contrary, Mother, it was all Tully and Sutton's idea—"

Mrs. Forrester forged full steam over her son's words. "Have you any idea what those cigars cost us? Not to mention your brother's bomb—a twelve-year-old with a talent for explosives!" She shook her head in disbelief. "We had to endow a four-year scholarship! Which, by the way, will be deducted from *your* trust funds."

"Really, Mother, it sounds as if Old Peterson was taking undue advantage—"

"You are not to refer to your headmaster as 'Old Peterson'!" Mrs. Forrester's substantial bosom rose and fell dramatically beneath her lace jabot. Her dark hair, coiled atop her head, bobbed as she paced the drawing room's Persian carpet. Her taffeta skirts rustled between rich furnishings and thick velvet draperies. "If only your father were here to manage this situation. But as he is off chasing butterflies—"

"He is not!" Miles stood straighter than his brother ever had. Cobalt eyes flashed behind his thick glasses as he shook his mop of black hair with vehemence. "His last letter *specifically* stated that he was on the verge of tracking down a variant of the Cambrian period trilobite in the uninhabited Los Roques Islands off the coast of Venezuela." Miles stopped to catch his breath. "And I wish I were with him!"

Mrs. Forrester threw up her hands. "Be that as it may. At the moment, your summer holidays are well in hand. As I intend both of you will be." She paused to make certain she had her sons' undivided attention. A painfully long moment passed.

"All right, Mother, what's the punishment?"

Mrs. Forrester trained her glare on Wick, then Miles. "Your *punishment* will be to accompany your Uncle Eustace—"

"*Uncle Eustace!*" gasped Wick.

"—to Europe." A grim smile crossed her face. "You will help your uncle purchase art —"

"*Art!*" Wick and Miles spat out the word simultaneously.

"Art." Mrs. Forrester's smile went rigid. "And hopefully become civilized in the process."

✣ ✣ ✣

"Not two days back in New York and already Mother is shipping me off again." Wick was draped across Miles's bed, bemoaning his fate.

"You're not the only one being banished. I have to go too," Miles pointed out.

"True enough." Wick ran his fingers through his dark hair, mussing its careful part. "Sometimes I wonder why our parents even bothered having us. Father's always off on expeditions, and Mother's got all her charity committees. I don't suppose it ever crossed her mind that charity could begin at home."

Miles shrugged. "What *were* you planning to do during vaca-tion, then?" He was systematically bundling small bottles of chemicals in cotton wadding and packing them in the steamer trunk that dwarfed his kneeling frame.

"Do?" Wick writhed at the thought of lost delights. "Some of the fellows and I were going to slip up to Saratoga and —"

"Lucky Mother doesn't know you play the horses with your allowance," Miles broke in. "Somehow I think that might go down worse than the cigars."

"How would she know? Unless a certain obnoxious little brother were to tell her."

"Peace." Miles lovingly nestled a microscope in a drawer of

the trunk. "We're going to have to live with each other for the next three months. And what about your packing? We're meeting Uncle Eustace on the ship *tomorrow*, after all."

Wick didn't move. "Let the servants do it. It amuses them and keeps them occupied."

Miles reached for a bottle he'd overlooked. He squinted at the label. "Nitric acid. Wouldn't want to forget that, would I?"

Wick snorted. "No, I guess you wouldn't. Not if you intend to blow up half of Europe."

"Scoffing is uncalled for. I haven't got the system quite perfected yet, is all. That little surprise I hooked up under the Latin master's chair never did work. It was only bad luck he dropped his chalk that day, and bent down to fetch it, and —"

"And noticed the wires sticking out. Horses are safer, dear brother."

"True," Miles grinned. "But a little explosion now and then is more fun."

✛ ✛ ✛

The next morning, bands played and confetti flew on the dock where the great ocean liner *New York* was berthed. Wick and Miles ignored it all as they tentatively approached their Uncle Eustace through the crowds.

He didn't appear all that daunting, to be sure. Of medium height and partially bald, he wore a conservative brown suit tailored to disguise his paunch. Eustace Forrester looked like the self-satisfied president of a small town bank. His eyes and his words, however, bespoke his calling.

"So. My nephews and heirs. The playboy and the pyromaniac."

Wick ignored the remark and thrust out his hand. "It's good to see you too, Uncle Eustace. How long has it been? Twenty million dollars ago? Thirty?"

"Would that it had been fifty million."

Eustace Forrester turned to stride up the gangplank as Wick's unshaken hand wilted. Apparently Uncle Eustace wasn't too thrilled by the arrangement either. The brothers shot each other slightly queasy glances, then boarded the ship.

✣ ✣ ✣

"That wasn't fair of him, Wick. It wasn't fair in the least!"

"What wasn't fair?" Wick was trying to get his bearings as they made their way through the labyrinthine passages of the ship. "The steward said our rooms were in this direction."

"Uncle Eustace calling me a pyromaniac. I've *never* had an irresistible urge to start fires! Fire isn't the purpose of my experiments at all—"

"Here's A Deck. Up this flight of stairs." Wick began climbing. "He's trying to get the upper hand from the start, Miles. A standard negotiating ploy. He wants it clear who's in charge." Wick halted before a polished oak door. "I'm more annoyed that no one gave us a farewell party. It *is* supposed to be traditional."

"What, you expected the coachman and the footman to share a bottle of champagne after dumping us on the dock?"

Wick sighed. "Our stock in the Forrester household isn't even that high."

He pulled the door open, revealing a compact yet elegant sitting room with a bedroom on either side. "Uncle Eustace's suite! Why can't we have our own staterooms?"

"Because you need looking after, obviously."

Both boys spun in the direction of the words. They were spoken by a slim, elegant man of indeterminate age. Sharp black eyes gleamed below hair that shone like patent leather. As the boys stared, his pencil-thin mustache twitched slightly above tight lips.

"Who are you?" Miles demanded.

He granted a faint nod. "Mr. Forrester's valet, general factotum, and adviser on matters of art. You may call me José Gregorio."

Miles poked his head into the water-chamber closet, then pulled it out again. "Are there any other servants to spy on us?"

"I assure you, Master Miles —it is Master Miles, is it not? I assure you that I will be adequate to the task."

Wick and Miles shared a shrug of defeat. It was evident they'd entered the enemy camp.

✧ ✧ ✧

Meals in the Grand Dining Saloon were served in assigned seats. Wick and Miles had been escorted to a small table for three. The two sat waiting for Uncle Eustace in a sea of anonymous diners, ivory and gold paneling, tapestries, and gilded figures of Neptune's court—all beneath a dome of sparkling mirrors.

Miles tugged at the collar of his stiff shirt front. "Who packed this monkey suit for me anyhow? I sure didn't!"

"The servants, little brother. The all-knowing, all-seeing servants."

"I'm fed up with servants. They're as bad as schoolmasters and room proctors. A fellow can't breathe with them around!"

"Why do you think our dear father spends most of his life in jungles, Miles? Didn't you ever wonder about that?"

"He loves discovering things the way I do, Wick."

"Some of that is true. But to my mind, escape is his primary motive —" Wick suddenly jumped to his feet. "Good evening, Uncle."

Miles followed suit as Eustace Forrester settled himself, picked up his menu, and gestured for them to sit. "I hope there's nothing too rich. My stomach won't stand for it. Ever since that last merger went sour . . ."

"Just two dozen oysters on the half shell, Uncle Eustace," Miles piped up. "And lobster with drawn butter, separated by a cream soup, followed by —"

Uncle Eustace clutched his stomach and groaned. "I can read, nephew!" He handed the menu to a hovering waiter. "Only a salad for me. And dry toast."

The waiter's eyebrows rose.

"Do try to keep my nephews' selections under cover. Merely the sight—"

It was a difficult meal. Miles was sneaking a bite of chocolate mousse into his mouth as his uncle finished the last of his dry toast and rose.

"I'll expect both of you in our suite within fifteen minutes. I wish to inaugurate a plan of study."

Wick spluttered over his coffee. "Study? It's summer! And there's a dance tonight . . ."

Uncle Eustace paused to extract a watch from his dinner jacket. "That would be in fourteen minutes."

⁜   ⁜   ⁜

"I could do it on my own, but as you two have been thrust upon me—" Uncle Eustace had changed into a lounging jacket and was pacing dyspeptically around the tiny sitting room.

"—I shall expect your cooperation and assistance. For all your obvious failings, I perceive inklings of intelligence. It would be too dismal a thought to presume that the family brains have been squandered on your generation, leaving the twentieth century rushing upon us bereft of functioning Forresters—"

Uncle Eustace burped, and José Gregorio rushed a glass of bromide into his outstretched hand. That downed, he spun on the young men.

"Accordingly, here is the battle strategy—"

"We need a battle strategy to visit Europe?" Miles spit out the words before he could stop himself. He clapped a hand over his mouth. Too late. Uncle Eustace favored him with a frown.

"For your information, nephew, we are not merely visiting Europe. *Anyone* can visit Europe. *We* are *invading* Europe. This is a search-and-seize operation, to acquire for our fair country the spoils it needs to uplift its citizenry!"

"What are we searching and seizing?" Wick considered that a reasonable question. Uncle Eustace did not.

"Surely your mother has apprised you of the situation. *Art.* Rembrandt, da Vinci, Michelangelo, Dürer. Rockefeller and

J. P. Morgan got 'em. I want 'em, too."

"I know about Rockefeller and Morgan"—Miles dared to speak again—"but I'm not sure who those others are. And how is getting them going to uplift our citizenry?"

"Because hereafter the masterworks of these great artists will reside on *our* side of the Atlantic. José Gregorio!" shouted Uncle Eustace.

The valet materialized from the bedroom. "Yes, sir?"

"The moment has arrived to prove your purported expertise. Bring the art folios. My nephews' boarding school has obviously been derelict in its duties."

✣ ✣ ✣

"*Yeech.*"

This was Miles's general opinion after a painful hour of study. "All these gods and goddesses floating around, doing silly things."

Wick was not impressed by the black-and-white photographs either. "Why would you want one of these murky things, Uncle? I'd say the Europeans are welcome to them. Why not something more interesting? My friend Sutton's family has a fantastic painting of a racehorse. Call it a 'Stubbs.' Now *that* I could understand. You can practically see its muscles pulse—"

"George Stubbs is not High Art. Rockefeller and J. P. Morgan have High Art—"

"So you want it too." Wick snapped shut the folio in his lap. "Apparently they bested you on that merger—"

"*No one* bests Eustace Forrester! The deal was merely a momentary setback. I'll soon have them where it hurts." He clutched at his stomach again. "Invading Europe is merely phase one of my grand plan. It also fulfills my doctor's orders to take the air. I shall return rejuvenated and triumphant."

"Has it ever occurred to you, Uncle," offered Wick, "that maybe Rockefeller and Morgan got all the High Art first?"

✣ ✣ ✣

"This is not going to work, Miles."

Four days into the voyage, Wick and Miles were leaning over the ship's railing staring blindly at gray, roiling waves.

"Uncle Eustace is obsessed. He's smothering us with all the energy he usually saves for his railroad mergers. Making us memorize the works of his precious painters and their provenances . . . "

"Actually, the provenance part is interesting, Wick." Miles wiped sea spray from his spectacles. "It's like playing detective, tracking down the history of who owned a picture. Uncle couldn't be doing it without José Gregorio either. Why, *he* knows exactly how Dürer signed his name, and what kind of pigments Rembrandt used—"

"Spare me your enthusiasm, Miles. Uncle hasn't given us a minute to ourselves."

"Actually, he's given us thirty minutes. Three times a day, to take exercise on deck."

"Why must you be so precise?" complained Wick.

Miles studied his pocket watch. "Because it's my nature. And because I'm afraid of what he'll do if we're late. We have nine minutes left of exercise time."

"What *can* he do? We're aboard a ship, after all—" Wick stopped as a thought occurred to him. "But we won't be on this ship forever, will we?" A sly smile played on his lips.

Miles frowned. "What are you plotting, Wick?"

"*Mutiny.* After we reach solid land. We'll go through the motions for a bit, until we get our bearings, then . . ." He pulled out a cigar secreted in his jacket and struggled to light it in the wind.

"Wick! Uncle Eustace will smell that! Where'd you get it anyway?"

Wick inhaled and coughed. "Matter of a suitable bribe to our room steward." He puffed and coughed again.

Miles wrinkled his nose. "You really like those disgusting things?"

"Loath 'em. But a fellow's got to show some spirit."

"I could think of better ways to do that."

"How, pray tell?"

"Blow up Uncle Eustace's art folios?"

"An appealing thought, little brother. But one must save such satisfying solutions for greater causes." Wick tossed the cigar into the ocean. "Maybe it would be best to pretend enthusiasm. It usually works on the masters at school just before marking period. Gets their defenses down." Wick turned to his brother. "What *delights* await us this afternoon?"

"The Flemish and German Schools."

Wick grinned. "All is not lost. Maybe there'll be a few good nudes. Those northerners seemed quite fond of Adam and Eve."

"Don't let Uncle Eustace catch you gawking, Wick."

"I won't. I've been watching how that José Gregorio does things. Suave, that's what he is. Just calmly points out the texture of a brush stroke, or—"

"Forget the brush strokes. I can't wait till we see these pictures in the flesh—in color!"

Wick cuffed his brother's head. "That's hardly the sort of education Mother had in mind for you."

Two

The ocean liner docked at Cherbourg after sunset. José Gregorio bundled his charges and their luggage onto a night train to Paris, and in the wee hours the groggy party arrived at the Grand Hotel. Much later that morning, Miles poked his brother awake.

"What is it?" Wick growled.

"Come look out from the balcony! We're in Paris! In France! The land of Pasteur, Lavoisier . . . "

Wick clamped a pillow over his head. "Wake me when we're back in New York."

There was a brisk knock at the door and Miles sprang to open it—to be shoved aside by a cart pushed by a white-jacketed waiter.

"*Le petit déjeuner, monsieur.*"

"Breakfast? Tremendous! I could eat an elephant!" Miles lifted the silver-plated cover, anticipating sausages and eggs, perhaps a steak or two. "What's this? *Rolls?*"

"*Croissants, monsieur.*"

"Hey, wait a minute—" But the waiter was already gone.

Miles sniffed at two steaming pots. "You'd better bite the bullet, Wick, and get up before the hot part of breakfast turns cold. And before I steal your share of this sumptuous repast."

Wick struggled from his covers and wandered over, hoisting his pajama bottoms. "Cocoa? And rolls with a little butter and jam? That's all?"

"I think you're supposed to mix the hot milk with the chocolate in these bowls, since there aren't any cups." Miles demonstrated and sipped. "It's very good cocoa. And the rolls are called *croissants*." He downed his share, then hunted for stray crumbs. "How do you suppose the French get through the day on only this?"

"Wine," Wick mumbled. "I read somewhere they drink wine like the very devil."

"Oh, say! Luncheon will be something to look forward to, then, won't it?"

Wick eyed his younger brother blearily. "You're not supposed to be enjoying any of this, Miles."

"But we're on solid land again. It's a glorious day." Miles pointed at the sunshine streaming through the French doors that opened onto their balcony. "And it's so different from New York, Wick. I saw people walking down the street carrying long loaves of bread under their arms. Just like that! I don't mind making plans for a mutiny, but in the meantime, I intend to enjoy myself!"

Wick snorted. "The surroundings may be different, but everything else is the same. We're still under the thumb of Uncle Eustace and his precious valet."

As if to prove his point, the double doors set within the panels of one wall slid open. José Gregorio appeared, perfect in dove-gray morning suit and spats.

"Excellent. The young masters have risen. Directly after you've finished your ablutions, present yourselves in the adjoining room. Your uncle is anxious to begin his 'invasion.'"

❖ ❖ ❖

An open landau and matched pair of horses conveyed the party down the Rue Royale, through the Place de la Concorde to the river Seine, then along its banks toward the great palace that housed the Louvre.

Miles bounced with excitement, scarcely knowing where to look first. "See those barges on the river, Wick? Wouldn't it be a lark to ride on one?"

"Along with the coal, I suppose." Wick's mood hadn't improved. He crossed his legs and flicked a speck of dust from his trousers. Then he faced his uncle, who was sitting opposite him, next to the valet. "Say, Uncle Eustace, isn't it about allowance time?"

The elder Forrester grunted. "It will be allowance time when you have proven your worth to our mutual enterprise."

"But a fellow can't walk about with empty pockets!" Wick turned one out. "Can he?"

"Your physical wants will be attended to, Chadwick. As the need arises. Beyond that, the subject is closed."

"I knew he'd smell that cigar smoke on you," Miles whispered in his brother's ear. "Hardly worth wasting all your pocket money—"

"You have something to say as well, Miles?"

"No, Uncle." He swung his head forward. "I have five dollars left from New York. As soon as I change it into French money, I'd like to check these stalls along the river. I think I spotted an engraving of Louis Pasteur that I'd love for my room back home—"

"*Humph.* We're hunting for finer stuff than that. And here we are." The carriage pulled to a stop. "I thought we'd observe the real thing before tomorrow's appointment with an art dealer who comes highly recommended."

✛ ✛ ✛

"Wow!" Miles exclaimed. "This museum really is a palace!"

"Well, it's not shabby." Wick was working hard not to be impressed by the opulence surrounding him.

José Gregorio consulted a small booklet he'd just purchased. "We go up these stairs to the *Grande Galerie*. That would be the picture gallery. I believe we can dispense with the Assyrian and Mesopotamian collections for the moment."

"They've got those too?"

"I assure you, Master Miles, the Louvre has nearly *everything*." He began to ascend.

Wick and Miles followed the valet, with Uncle Eustace puffing in the rear.

"Where'd they get it all?" Miles asked.

"The core of the collection belonged to the great kings of France, but it's been considerably augmented by Napoleonic wars and general pillage."

"Oh." Miles considered the implications as they entered the vast hallway lit by skylights. "Sort of like us, I suppose. The pillage part, at least."

"We've not come to sack and burn, Master Miles," José Gregorio said. "Your uncle's acquisitions will be legitimate purchases from somewhat impoverished nobility. If anything we'll be doing them a service." He paused as the mass of paintings filling nearly every inch of the long corridor's walls overwhelmed them.

"Say, I wouldn't mind taking home something like this!" Wick halted before a vibrant scene of cardplayers—one hiding aces behind his back, obviously cheating.

"Merely a genre piece," sniffed José Gregorio.

"Still and all . . . " Wick lingered by the painting.

"This"—the valet moved on—"is the quality we seek. The *Mona Lisa*, by the greatest of all masters, Leonardo da Vinci!"

Wick caught up and inspected the picture. "Well, she does look better than in those wretched photographs you showed us on the ship," he allowed.

Uncle Eustace cleared his throat and spoke for the first time. "Her expression . . . she looks like she's just done a deal for the Union Pacific and the Central Pacific Railroads both—with the

Atchison, Topeka, and Santa Fe thrown in for good measure!"

"Study it," commanded José Gregorio. "Taste it, as you might taste the finest of wines. *Feel* the spirituality of *La Gioconda*. Walk into the mysterious landscape behind her. . . ."

While the others were studying the picture, Miles was studying José Gregorio. He was more interesting than any old mysterious landscape. "You haven't always been a valet, have you?" he blurted out.

José Gregorio abruptly turned from the da Vinci. "There's also a Vermeer to see. And a fine self-portrait by Dürer. He was quite young when he made the likeness, and it should appeal to you gentlemen."

The group finally stopped before the promised Dürer.

"Albrecht Dürer was about nineteen when he painted this self-portrait in 1493, just before his marriage," José Gregorio explained. "It was probably a wedding gift to his fiancée, Agnes."

"How'd you come to know that?" Miles asked.

He shrugged. "A simple matter. You'll notice the young Dürer has a few whiskers sprouting on his chin. Beards weren't fashionable in his day, but he later grew one—perhaps in protest, or maybe as a sort of vanity to set himself off from the common crowd. It did make him look remarkably like Jesus Christ."

Wick rubbed his smooth chin, as if contemplating a similar act of protest should his beard ever choose to sprout.

"And then," continued the valet, pointing to Dürer's hands, "he is holding a sprig of the flower eryngium—a symbol of conjugal fidelity."

"What does that mean?" Miles wanted to know.

"It means being faithful to his new wife, dummy," Wick answered.

"Oh." Miles studied the portrait. "I think he liked clothes as much as you do, Wick." Miles adjusted his glasses and leaned closer. "And he looks like an interesting person . . . as if he's hiding a whole bunch of secrets, but he's not about to let on. Not to just *anybody*." Miles continued to stare intently. "I'd like to see some more of this Albrecht Dürer's pictures."

"Alas," José Gregorio mourned, "there is not much else in Paris. Most of Dürer's work has been dispersed, some of it lost forever."

Uncle Eustace was consulting his pocket watch. "Isn't it time for luncheon yet? Somehow looking at all these things I can't buy has given me an appetite for the first time in days."

"Certainly, sir," the valet responded. "Fine pictures can only be appreciated for a short length of time, in small quantities. Otherwise one might become satiated."

✣ ✣ ✣

Uncle Eustace and José Gregorio shared a bottle of wine over luncheon. Wick and Miles were delighted when the waiter presented them with wine glasses as well. Their delight was short-lived.

"None for them," Uncle Eustace ordered the waiter. "*Rien.* That's how you say it, isn't it, José Gregorio?"

"Your pronunciation is excellent, sir."

"Please, Uncle," Wick begged. "When in Rome, one ought to—"

"This is not Rome, Chadwick. And your mother reminds me with dreary regularity of her Temperance Society presidency. Speaking of whom, I trust you have already posted a letter to her?"

Wick sighed. "It's my turn this week, Miles's next." He settled his elbows on the table and sank his chin into his upheld hands. "A European education is supposed to be stimulating, Uncle Eustace. You're hardly giving us a chance."

"I'm afraid you'll have to settle for the stimulation of art, nephew, while you're in my charge."

✣ ✣ ✣

Free at last in the privacy of their hotel room that evening, Wick tore off his coat and tie. "There is no way I can put up with another three months of this!"

Miles was counting the small pile of franc notes he'd acquired that afternoon. "Things seem to be fairly inexpensive here, Wick, but this won't take us far." He wadded the money and stuffed it in a pocket. "What else can we do? José Gregorio is holding our return tickets—and he's not about to let them out of his hands."

"There must be a way." Wick cast off his celluloid collar, then his shirt. "If we could only talk Uncle out of some of his precious money. Heaven knows, he's got more than he knows what to do with." Wick paused. "All that lovely loot. Wasted on a man with no imagination."

"What would you do with it?"

"Buy horses," Wick promptly answered. "Set up a racing stable. If I started right now, I might have a contender for the Kentucky Derby in four years. Just think. . . ." His eyes turned dreamy. "Having a Derby entry for 1900, the beginning of a magnificent new century!"

"You'd train them? You don't even like to get your hands dirty!"

Wick returned to reality. "You hire people for that, feather-brain. You can hire people for practically anything. If you have enough money."

Miles studied his brother. "But don't you want to do anything yourself? Be really good at something? Better than the servants? Better even than José Gregorio?"

Wick settled onto his bed with a sigh. "Nobody could be better than José Gregorio."

"So why is he wasting his time valeting for Uncle Eustace?"

Wick cast a sharp glance toward his brother. "A good question, Miles. A very good question, indeed."

✣ ✣ ✣

The following morning brought another glorious Parisian June day, but Wick and Miles saw little of its glory. They were sequestered with Uncle Eustace and his art dealer, Pierre Polisson.

Dapper and lithe, Monsieur Polisson glided around the marble floors of his gallery, stopping before a painting to brush his lavish mustache or caress his auburn goatee. Matching waved hair swept back from his forehead to fall dramatically over his open Byronic collar. In lieu of a morning coat, a satin-lined cape swung from his shoulders.

Wick admired the theatrical dash of the man, though he was a little suspicious of the over-generous smiles. Then there were Polisson's eyes. A certain hunger—or perhaps deviousness—lodged in them. Wick glanced at his brother.

"Remember that study Father did on vultures?" Miles whispered, reading his mind.

Wick grinned in agreement as Polisson spoke.

"This is, indeed, your lucky day, Mr. Forrester! A courier has recently brought me a noteworthy painting. I have been studying it every spare moment, breathing in its masterful style, its rare northern opulence." Polisson's cape swirled. "I offer to you a genuine masterwork by none other than Lucas Cranach the Elder!" He swept to a curtained easel in the center of the gallery.

"Feast your eyes!"

Wick and Miles gasped as the covering fell away.

"That would be Cranach of the sixteenth-century German School, wouldn't it?" Wick inquired, spellbound by the very lush and very naked young woman revealed.

Miles pulled a magnifying glass from his pocket and stepped closer.

"Your nephews have taste, Mr. Forrester. *The Nymph of the Spring* does not come on the market just *any* day. Feast your own eyes, sir."

Uncle Eustace was, in fact, shielding his eyes. José Gregorio gently pulled his employer's hand away. "It's not the ultimate Cranach, of course, but it's a good beginning, sir."

A hesitant foot moved forward, followed by the portly stomach. "But where could I possibly hang her?"

"In your dining room, Uncle," Wick suggested. "It would improve your meals enormously."

Polisson's lips parted in a smile. "The young gentleman has been well educated. See how he has noticed Cranach's fine German town in the far background, the trickle of spring water down the crag in the closer distance, the two game birds nestled by the nymph's feet."

Wick's eyes were, in fact, riveted elsewhere.

Miles moved the magnifying glass over the canvas. "I *knew* these pictures would look better in color," he murmured.

Pierre Polisson stroked his goatee. "An absolute find. No question. Next to Dürer's *Adam and Eve*, Cranach created the most enticing human forms. There are so few still available. . . . And this one can be yours for a very reasonable figure."

"How reasonable?" Uncle Eustace asked with suspicion.

"A gentleman of your stature would never lower himself to bourgeois bargaining." The dealer gestured toward the easel. "Rockefeller would gladly pay a hundred thousand for a painting like this."

"Francs?" asked Wick.

Polisson frowned. "*Dollars*, young man."

Uncle Eustace was frowning too. The price was exorbitant, of course; yet it had been mentioned in the same breath as the name of his greatest rival.

"I have merely to cable Mr. Rockefeller," continued Polisson. "He's been on the lookout for a Cranach."

Uncle Eustace humphed and turned away. "Cover her, if you please, while I consider. She seems to be distracting my nephews. What else have you to show me?"

"Since you mentioned him, any Dürers?" Miles piped up.

Polisson focused on the boy in surprise. "I have come into a woodcut from his *Mary* series—" He stopped, considered Uncle Eustace carefully, and almost visibly made a decision before continuing. "Then again, I might have a line on something quite rare. . . . "

"What?" Wick inquired.

"One of Dürer's *Knot* woodcuts. From a series of six, created during his first visit to Italy. It's said they show strange and curious configurations of arabesques inspired by the great Leonardo. Although, for myself, I suspect the designs have astrological meaning." Noting interest in Uncle Eustace's eyes, as well as the boys', he continued. "There's talk—perhaps mere gossip—that a cache of Dürer's works may still be hidden in Nuremberg, his home. . . . Nothing must be discounted. I have feelers out to a member of the Dürerbund—"

"Dürerbund?" Wick asked.

Polisson lowered his voice. "A most mysterious German secret society, whose very existence is known only to a few—"

"Let's deal with the known here," barked Uncle Eustace. "What about da Vinci?"

The dealer shrugged, and the moment passed. "I do have a small drawing indisputably by Leonardo's hand."

Uncle Eustace glanced at the boys. "Why don't you two get yourselves some lunch while we continue here?"

Wick upended an empty pocket, and Uncle Eustace nodded to his valet. "Give them some dining money, will you?"

❖ ❖ ❖

"Why do you suppose Uncle Eustace let us out of his sight, Wick?"

The boys had bolted from Polisson's gallery to a *bistro* some blocks away. Now they lounged outdoors in the sunshine, sipping a cool white wine and nibbling omelettes.

"Trying to keep us away from any more nudes, I suspect. For a grown man, he's an incredible prude." Wick rolled a little wine on his tongue. "On the dry side, but with a pleasant touch of fruit, wouldn't you say?"

"Never tasted the stuff before, so I wouldn't know. I was wondering about the fermentation process though. If I could get a look at one of these French wineries, I'd bet I could concoct something in the science laboratory back at school."

Wick chuckled. "Finally something worthy of your talents, little brother." He patted his trousers pocket. "Good old José slipped me a big enough wad to dine comfortably at Maxim's. If we subtract the cost of this modest meal—"

"And hang onto the difference—" suggested Miles.

"And hang onto the difference," Wick repeated, "we've a good start on mutiny money, which could increase, assuming José's generosity on lunches continues."

Miles took a sizable swallow from his glass. "So, have you formulated any actual plans?"

"I have, indeed." Wick slathered butter on a piece of crusty bread. "How far away do you suppose Nuremberg is? I never paid much attention to geography, I'm afraid."

"Strange you should mention Nuremberg." Miles was beginning to feel exceptionally expansive.

Wick amply refilled their glasses from the half-empty wine bottle. "The way I see things, we have a potentially winning situation here. We have the possibility of conducting our little revolt *and* proving ourselves in the process."

"Could you be referring to tracking down certain lost Dürer woodcuts?"

"Indeed." Wick smiled contentedly. "I sort of liked the fellow's looks yesterday at the Louvre. Completely self-assured. On top of his destiny. My sort of guy."

"And if you can believe Polisson, Dürer comes with a genuine secret society too." Miles downed a fluffy bite of his omelette.

"If we could locate his *Knot* series, it would be quite a coup," Wick observed.

"True," Miles agreed a bit fuzzily. "It being so rare and all."

"Doesn't matter what the prints actually look like. Who really cares? Even Uncle Eustace would have to stand up and salute."

"Get some respect for a change." Miles reached for his glass. "Think *we'll* be able to stand up after all this wine? And walk?" He belched discreetly. "At least as far as that bookseller's near the gallery. Pick up a few maps."

"No problem. And an excellent idea, dear brother. Maybe we

ought to buy a French dictionary too. Not to mention a few guide-books to places such as Germany. Start researching our Great Escape."

Wick reached for the bottle and tipped it until it was absolutely dry.

Three

"You do it," Miles insisted. "You're the oldest. It will sound more reasonable coming from you."

Wick nodded. "We may as well use José Gregorio's talents."

Squaring his shoulders, he knocked on the sliding door separating their room from their uncle's suite. After receiving no response he edged it open. José Gregorio was emerging from the bathroom on the far side of the sitting area, steam haloing his shirtsleeved form rather angelically—or was it demonically? Wick cleared his throat.

The valet started. "Master Wick!"

"Uncle's not around, is he?"

"He's just begun his bath. I anticipate a long soak after the strain of purchasing all that art from Polisson today."

"Good." Wick stepped into the room. "I mean, it was you I really wanted to chat with."

José Gregorio slipped into his jacket. "If I may be of service."

"Well, Miles and I were thinking . . . " Wick hesitated, not in the habit of asking for either work or favors. He finally rushed into his request before he lost his nerve. "Would you consider giving us a few French lessons?"

"I thought the young masters had no need for anything but *American*."

Wick stiffened. "Maybe we have been a bit shortsighted. There do seem to be other cultures, other functioning languages in the world, and—"

"You actually might have the need to utilize them?"

"In fact, yes," Wick admitted. "I took a bit of German at school, of course, and Latin. But neither stayed too well."

José Gregorio pottered about the room, straightening things that really didn't need to be straightened. "So I surmised."

"Say, be a pal. Give us a break!"

The valet paused from his labors to smile. "Was that a *please* I heard?"

Miles popped into the room. "Yes, it was. *Please* will you give us some French lessons? We need to know more about Dürer too, and—"

José Gregorio raised his hands in mock defeat. "It's only a question of asking nicely. My services are at your command."

"Not like that," Wick protested. "None of this servant-master nonsense. We'd really appreciate it if you'd help us out, man to man."

"*Merci beaucoup. Tout de suite, à votre chambre.*"

"Come again?" Wick asked.

Miles grabbed his arm. "In our room, Wick. At once. Hurry up!"

✢ ✢ ✢

During the next two weeks in Paris, Wick and Miles prepared for their escape. As their French lessons progressed, they chafed less at the daily rounds of sightseeing—usually concluding with a visit to Pierre Polisson's gallery. And during each visit, the dealer tempted his American millionaire with another little treasure.

"That Pierre certainly has a lot of stuff squirreled away," Miles commented one evening while setting up a Bunsen burner.

"True." Wick glanced up from the map he was studying. "What are you doing with those tubes and glass piping?"

"I decanted a small sample of wine from lunch today. I'm going to distill it and analyze the alcohol content. Got to keep my skills in shape."

"Oh." Wick considered the experiment briefly. "But Polisson's art must be all right, because José has given most of it his blessing. At least on technique and authenticity. He hasn't commented on the prices Uncle's paying."

"It's only money." Miles shrugged. He pulled the cork from a miniature beaker and carefully drained the contents into a waiting tube. "I bet Pierre Polisson will have more fun spending it than Uncle Eustace ever would." He reached for his brother's jacket draped over a nearby chair, dug out a match, and carefully lit his apparatus. "I think my favorite after Cranach's *Nymph of the Spring* is that Botticelli *Virgin and Child* Uncle bought today. It's got a really terrific donkey and cow."

"You could have *asked* for a match before pawing through my jacket," Wick complained. "But you're right. The donkey was particularly poignant. It almost makes me sorry we've decided to escape before Uncle goes to Florence next week. José says they've got some fabulous Botticellis in the Uffizi Gallery. He says they've got a *Birth of Venus*—she sort of rises from the waves on this huge clamshell—that'd make you never want to look at another Cranach nude again."

"Hmmm." Miles's forehead creased in thought. "If that's the case. . . . Dürer did visit Italy himself on two separate trips. And we do need to get more clues about him if we want to find that missing cache of woodcuts. . . . "

Wick returned his attention to the map. "In point of fact, Florence isn't that much farther from Nuremberg than Paris is. Almost equidistant. I suppose we might consider tagging along for another few days. The extra lunch money wouldn't hurt either. . . . "

A discreet knock sounded through the sliding door. Miles

ignored it to study the faint line of condensation beginning to form inside his piping. Wick stuffed the maps under his bedclothes.

"Lesson time. Drag yourself from that experiment and sharpen up, Miles. We may need to learn some Italian next."

✣ ✣ ✣

With mixed feelings the boys boarded a night train bound for Italy from the *Gare de l'Est*. Wick shoved his overnight bag into the cubicle the two would share. "There can't possibly be as many cathedrals in Italy as France."

"Don't bet on it, Wick. Religion seems to be a sort of European sport. See who can build the biggest churches, then see who can kill off the most people on the opposite team. I did like St. Denis today, though. The cathedral was ugly as sin, but all those bodies!"

Miles squeezed into the tiny space next to his brother. "Who would've thought they stashed dead bodies inside churches? And who would've thought we'd get to see the exact spot where Pepin the Short was buried? From ages ago! Or all those other ancient French kings and queens?"

"Who'd have cared?" Wick pummeled his case into an overhead rack, then reached for his brother's.

"You haven't quite developed the correct attitude, Wick. Hey! Take it easy with my satchel!"

Wick gave it another good shove. "Why?"

Miles stared up at the bag for a long moment, as if waiting for something to happen. When nothing did, he let out his breath. "I've got most of my chemistry kit in there. In case of eventualities. You wouldn't want to break any of those bottles."

Wick eyed Miles's bag. "*You'll* shove it up next time. With me waiting in the corridor."

Miles shrugged and turned his attention to the little door that led directly from their sleeper onto the station platform. He snapped the shade up and down, then experimentally opened and shut the door.

"Isn't this funny? Not at all like the Pullman cars back home. Our own private escape route. In our own private room. If we hadn't already decided to hang on through Florence, we could disappear with Uncle never knowing which stop we'd skipped from."

Wick was showing more interest in his brother than in the door. "Sometimes, Miles, you exhibit cunning far beyond my expectations."

✣ ✣ ✣

Miles was allotted the top berth that night, so *he'd* be nearest to his lethal satchel. He was delighted. Climbing into the bed after dinner, Miles bounced, tossed, and finally slid down to the floor.

"What are you doing?" Wick asked from the lower berth.

"Opening the window shades so I can watch the scenery pass by."

"It's dark, ninny. You won't be able to see a thing."

"I'll be able to see lights in villages and the mountains when we get to them." Miles flipped up the shades, then pattered to the corridor door.

"Where are you going?"

"Need a glass of water."

"Good night, then." Wick pulled a blanket over his head.

✣ ✣ ✣

Miles darted back just as Wick was drifting into sleep.

"Wick. Wick!" He shook his brother.

"Now what!"

"Remember how you used to be pretty decent at playing cards?"

Wick groaned, sat up, and cracked his head on the berth above. "This had better be good, Miles."

"In the dining car. They've cleared the tables, and a bunch of men are playing cards. I'm not sure, but it looks like poker. For wagers."

"Poker?" Wick instantly turned alert. "How much have we got saved?"

"More than twenty-five dollars in francs. José Gregorio's

been pretty free with lunch money lately."

Wick reached for his shirt and trousers. "That should be just about enough to get into the game. Hand me my jacket and tie."

"You're really going to do it? Take a chance on losing our entire nest egg?"

Wick was already fumbling with his tie. "It was your idea, brother. Don't go weak-kneed on me."

"I wouldn't consider it. As long as you win." Miles grinned.

Wick was at the door. "What about Uncle and José?"

"No lights in their compartments. I think it's safe."

"If you want to watch you'll have to change out of your pajamas." Wick poked his head into the corridor. "And for heaven's sake, don't talk to me while I'm playing. I need total focus."

✢ ✢ ✢

By the time Miles joined his brother, Wick had inserted himself into the game. Most of the players were puffing at cigars. Wick had one clamped between his teeth too, but it wasn't lit. He was obviously serious about that focus business. Little piles of franc notes were piled in front of the players, as well as a large bottle of brandy. An untouched glass of cognac sat before Wick.

Miles hovered in the shadows, nervously watching. His brother's skill at poker was a legend at school, yet these competitors were grown men. Even so, the chance to increase their mutiny funds was irresistible.

A card was rejected and another accepted from the dealer. A beefy man, tie askew, flung down two. Then it was Wick's turn. He discarded *three*. . . . Not promising. Not promising at all. Someone made a remark and chuckled. Miles's French was not good enough to catch anything but the suggestion of an insult. Wick was oblivious. Apparently satisfied, he reshuffled the five cards he was holding.

With the next round of discards, betting began. This time Wick asked for only one card. Miles brightened. That was a positive sign. More wagering. . . . The hand was called. Wick set down three kings and two tens. He took the pot.

Miles pulled up a chair outside the circle and settled in for a long night. That first sign of satisfaction on Wick's face was never repeated—yet he won nearly every hand. The pile of money before him grew. His fellow players—several French, one German, and a probable Italian—bit harder into their cigars. They swallowed more often from their glasses. They did not look happy.

Miles began getting worried. He glanced at his pocket watch in the flickering light of the car. It was already well past two in the morning. He watched as Wick took yet another pot. The Frenchman across the table flung down his cards.

"*Vous trichez!*"

Miles's vocabulary may not have been broad, but anyone could understand that. Even Wick.

"I beg to differ," Wick protested. "I am *not* cheating!"

The Frenchman struggled from his seat. "*C'est vrai!*"

The Italian pulled at him, to no avail.

"*Tricheur!*" The Frenchman leaned across the table and grabbed Wick's lapels. The unsmoked cigar fell from his lips.

"Nuts to orders!" Miles lunged to his brother's defense but instead tripped over his chair. A mysterious hand roughly hauled him to his feet.

"Who—"

A spate of rapid French burst from the shadowed form behind Miles. He twisted to see—

"José Gregorio!"

The valet had thrown a smoking jacket over his night-clothes and a silk scarf around his neck. His hair was uncharacteristically tousled, but his eyes burned bright. His free hand held a neat little pearl-handled revolver pointed directly at the disgruntled poker player. The Frenchman backed off.

"Wick! Collect your winnings instantly. You're out of the game."

Wick reached for his brandy glass and downed its contents with *élan*. "Certainly."

He stuffed the pile of notes into his pockets and rose, nodding around the table. "Thank you, gentlemen. Quite an interesting evening."

"Wick!"

The valet dropped Miles to collar his brother. Wick marched off, grinning and unrepentant, with Miles bringing up the rear.

✛ ✛ ✛

"What am I going to do with the two of you?"

They were packed into the boys' compartment. Miles pulled out his watch again. Two-fifty-five. He stifled a yawn. "Will you tell Uncle?"

Wick tried a different approach. "Want to share our winnings?"

José Gregorio's glare could have ignited a fire. He jammed his revolver into a pocket and ran a hand through his hair. "You haven't a clue yet, either of you. Have you?"

"A clue to what?" Wick asked.

"Is this some sort of mystery? Or is it a test?" Miles wanted to know. "Because if it's a test, maybe we could continue it in the morning, after we get some sleep."

"No. Sit!"

Miles and Wick crowded onto the bottom berth. It was a tight fit.

"Move over, Wick!"

"I'm moved as far as I can go. Move yourself!"

"*Gentlemen!*" The valet spat out the word. "I thought we were making some progress with the lessons, but apparently I was mistaken."

"To the contrary," Wick countered. "I was able to catch quite a bit of the small talk around the table this evening—"

"That is not the sort of progress to which I was referring!" The valet paced two steps—the length of the cabin—and back again. "I supposed we were making some progress toward your moral and ethical education. Obviously my hopes were premature."

"I don't see what's wrong with playing a little poker," Wick protested. "And besides, it was Miles's idea. He spotted the game—"

"I have no interest in who was responsible. I want to know why you joined that game in the first place, Wick."

"Why, to win some pocket money, of course! Uncle's been a regular miser—"

"And if you had failed, had gone into debt? Had you stopped to consider who would have bailed you out? Your uncle? He'd sooner see both of you in reform school!" The valet completed three lengths of the cabin and back.

"More to the point, did you stop to consider what might have happened had I not rescued you from that angry Frenchman?"

"But you did. And besides, I rarely lose." Wick couldn't disguise the slight swagger in his voice. "It's a matter of concentrating, considering the mathematical odds—and natural luck with cards."

"He's right," Miles agreed. "All the fellows at school owe him money—"

"Enough!" The valet planted himself firmly before Wick. "Do you plan to spend the rest of your life frittering away your talents on such nonsense? Or will you learn to use those talents honestly, by the sweat of your brow? To *work* for something worthwhile?"

"Obviously, you've never played poker, José. That *was* work tonight."

"I have played poker. And it's not the sort of work I mean." He shook his head. "It's time to take a hard accounting of yourself, young man. Before it's too late." He spun and stopped at the door. "And no, I shall not report this incident to your uncle. At least for the moment. He has enough pain with his ulcers. Both of you, however, will be accountable to *me* in the future." With that, José Gregorio stalked out.

"Phew." Miles wiped his brow. "You certainly got him upset. What do you suppose he meant by that last comment?

Blackmail? And what are you going to do now?"

Wick eased up from his cramped seat. "First I'm going to count the loot. Then I'm going to get some sleep."

Four

Florence baked beneath the hot summer sun. Wick flung his linen jacket over a chair outside the tiny café on the edge of the Piazza della Signoria. He clawed open his collar and sat down.

"Don't understand why we have to wear all these clothes in the heat anyway. The Italians don't wear them. They're mostly in shirtsleeves, and rolled-up ones at that."

Miles unbuttoned his own jacket. "I thought you preferred sartorial elegance." He leaned back in his seat and tipped the brim of his straw boater to cut the glare. "But go ahead, strip as naked as Michelangelo's *David* for all I care."

"I should," Wick grumbled. "Just to show them. A fellow can't be elegant when he's all sweaty. Even my trouser creases have gone limp."

"Show who? Uncle? Or is it José Gregorio you're still mad at for his lecture the other night?"

Wick ignored the question. "What's Uncle's problem anyhow? Is he beginning to miss his mergers back home? He's been galloping us back and forth over the Arno River at top speed. The

Pitti Palace, the Convent of San Marco, the Uffizi twice. Not that I'm complaining about the Uffizi Gallery. We finally got to see a real Cranach *Adam and Eve*, not to mention *four* new Dürer paintings. And Botticelli's *Venus* was an eye-opener—"

"Won't talk about our dear valet, eh? Some of his words must have struck home. He won't just go away, you know."

"He's a *servant*, Miles," Wick sniffed. "Why should I care what he says?"

Miles tipped his hat lower. "You know he's not like any valet we've ever met. Uncle hired him for his expertise in art too. He's more than a servant."

"More *what* exactly?" complained Wick. "And what does he want from me? Would he rather I were out on this piazza, pushing a broom around?"

"I don't think he had that in mind with his 'sweat of the brow' comment. More in the way of working on your conscience . . . although what precisely a conscience is, I haven't figured out." Miles paused to locate a handkerchief and mop perspiration from his face. "Do you suppose it's connected to the soul? And how can you prove the existence of the soul anyhow? Scientifically, it's impossible. There's nothing to dissect, nothing to put under a microscope."

Across the table, Wick fanned himself with his Baedeker guidebook to northern Italy. "You've been trotted through too many churches lately. It's beginning to prey on your mind."

"The churches didn't do it. Maybe it was that crazy fifteenth-century monk's hair shirt we saw yesterday. Savonarola. Some conscience he must have had. Torching half the masterpieces of the Italian Renaissance! He deserved his hair shirt. Still . . . " Miles winced. "Imagine it next to the skin in this heat . . . "

"Here come our lemonades at last." Wick perked up. "Wine is all fine and good; but when you're truly hot and thirsty, there's nothing like a big, icy glass of lemonade."

Miles drank deeply, then grinned in agreement. "You don't even miss the fourteen percent alcohol content."

❖ ❖ ❖

"We never asked José about that gun, Wick."

"What gun?" Wick was sprawled across his bed during the afternoon's siesta. "Oh, the little pearl-handled special." He snorted. "A toy."

"It convinced your card partners fast enough. Who would've thought José packed a gun? Or that he'd know the precise moment it would be needed?"

"He probably just got up to use the WC and stumbled across us."

"Do you carry a revolver to wander down train corridors to the bathroom at night, Wick?"

Wick scowled. "Maybe he's always got it with him. Even this minute as he putters around Uncle's room."

Lying flat on his own bed, Miles stared at cracks in the ceiling above his head. "Maybe he's got unseen enemies pursuing him to the ends of the earth. Maybe he's play-acting at being a valet. You know, in disguise." Was that a spider in the center of the cracks, the center of the web? Miles readjusted his spectacles.

"That's ridiculous, Miles."

"Do you suppose Uncle is aware of the gun? Knows where José came from? We don't know *anything* about him."

"I don't care. Isn't this situation absurd enough for you? Being forced to take naps as if we were infants, while time is wasting away? We could be enroute to Nuremberg. Hot on the trail of those missing Dürers." Wick rubbed his chin. "I've been thinking about Albrecht's self-portrait at the Louvre. Sort of mysterious, and daring at the same time."

"Strange," Miles murmured. "I had the identical impression. And his little *Madonna of the Pear* at the Uffizi had that same secret feeling. Kind of whets your appetite for more." He propped himself on an elbow. "In fact, we might have enough cash right now to take off for Nuremberg. If used wisely that bundle from the card game could get us—"

A loud crash cut Miles short. He jumped as the adjoining door to their uncle's room sprang open and Eustace Forrester himself staggered through the doorway.

"José Gregorio!" he cried. "That linguine with cream sauce was a big mistake. Where did you put my medicine?"

Wick leaped to support their uncle's sagging body. "What's the matter with your leg, sir?"

"Gout! A nasty bout just hit me. First time in years. On top of the stomach . . . " He peered around anxiously. "Where *is* José Gregorio?"

"Last seen settling you down for your nap, Uncle Eustace," Wick assured him.

"He can't be far, Uncle," Miles added. "Probably down the hall using the facilities, or making arrangements with our landlady for dinner." Miles stopped and caught his brother's eye. "Maybe we'd best get Uncle Eustace into bed, then hunt for José."

"Right. I'll get him there, you do the searching . . . . That's it, Uncle Eustace, lean against me. Mind the doorway. Just a few more steps . . . "

His uncle slumped onto the waiting bed, and Wick plumped the pillows solicitously. "Just settle back and relax now."

"Stop fussing and get out of my sight!" Uncle Eustace snapped. "It's José I want. He knows how to make everything better!"

"I understand, I really do." Wick smoothed a sheet over his uncle's legs anyway, and was rewarded with a thought. "Where did you find him?"

Uncle Eustace slapped Wick's hands away. "Advertised. For a valet with *culture*. Offered top dollar. Just before the trip. My old valet Barton's rheumatics inconveniently forced his retirement, and José's references were impeccable. Why are you still hanging about? Stay out of my sight until I'm feeling better. That goes for your brother too! How your mother ever managed to saddle me with the two of you . . . "

Wick beat a hasty retreat.

⁜ ⁜ ⁜

"He can't have disappeared just like that," Miles wailed. "It's impossible!"

Hours later, Wick and Miles were no longer bored. They were frantic.

"A servant doesn't take off without notice, Miles. It's unprofessional."

"When are you going to stop thinking of José as a servant, Wick? You know he was much more than that, was *beyond* that—"

"You needn't use the *past* tense. Surely it's a bit premature." Wick sat nervously tapping a foot. "That doctor we fetched has been in there with Uncle Eustace for an awfully long time—"

"*Signores?*" The doctor nudged open the connecting door.

Miles hopped up. "Yes, Doctor? How is Uncle Eustace?"

The gentleman set down his bag and closed the door behind him. "He must rest in the bed. For many days. A fortnight, *sì*? And the food must be, how do you say it? Dull?"

"Bland," Wick offered.

"Ah. *Bland.* I will inform Signora Bellini. Also I will order a nurse. To keep the uncle comfortable. No?"

"Yes!" breathed Wick. "Yes, please."

"Otherwise, he should not be troubled. I return from time to time—"

Wick stood. "That would be excellent. Er . . . about your fee?"

The doctor patted a pocket. "Not to be worried. The uncle has found for me the retainer."

"Better and better." Wick ran a hand through his hair. "Do you really believe we shouldn't disturb him during this period?"

"The uncle only worries for his missing servant. Even he asks if the *polizia* should be called. This I tell him would not be a good thing. The *polizia* . . . " the doctor shrugged. "They confuse things, no? Besides, a good nursing sister from the convent will order all. Like the general of an army."

"Perfect." Wick smiled.

The doctor shared the smile. "For you also, to keep a distance might be wisdom." He cleared his throat. "The uncle seemed . . ."— he hesitated—"seemed quite *strong* in his desire for the solitude from his nephews. Ulcers, the gout. . . they make a man *difficult*. Give him the evil temper."

"They certainly do." Wick offered his hand. The doctor clasped it with enthusiasm and made his departure.

Wick collapsed onto his bed. "What time is it, Miles?"

"After six. José's been gone more than four hours. As far as we know. And he's certainly not anywhere in these lodgings. I've gone through the entire place with Signora Bellini. Even the attic."

"No one saw him leave," continued Wick. "No one saw anyone suspicious arrive."

"How could they? They were all resting through the heat of the day, Wick. Like us."

"So where is he? Where do we look next?"

Miles straightened his bedcovers, then began picking up discarded clothing strewn across the floor. "Probably in his room. Maybe he left a note or a clue."

"You just said you checked all the rooms while I was hunting down the doctor—"

"Only for a look, Wick. Not a proper *search*."

"Right, then. We'll continue the search."

✣   ✣   ✣

José Gregorio's tiny room was at the other end of the second-floor hallway from their uncle's. Wick twisted the doorknob tentatively, then gave the door a shove. Slowly, it squeaked open. A spartan bed, a straight-backed chair, and a time-blackened wardrobe filled the space.

"It looks as if he never even slept here," Miles said.

"I'm not sure he *ever* slept. But if he did, the maid's already tidied up." Wick crossed the threshold. "Where are his suitcases?" He opened the wardrobe. "Here's his morning suit. Neatly pressed. And his tweeds, smoking jacket, and scarf. What was he wearing this morning?"

"A white linen touring suit, like us."

Wick examined the bottom shelf. "Three pair of shoes, highly polished. His shaving kit. A bottle of that cologne he uses. A pristine pile of underwear . . . "

Miles was foraging under the bed. He pulled out a large suitcase. "This must be the rest of his stuff. I don't think he had a steamer trunk."

Wick left the wardrobe and helped spring the two clasps. Together, they opened the top of the suitcase.

"Well." Miles sank back on his heels. "What do you make of this?"

"Books," Wick answered. He shuffled through them. "No pearl-handled pistol in evidence."

"Somehow that makes me feel a little better. As if he's got some protection, wherever he is . . ."

Wick picked up one of the books. "Maybe this will tell us something." He read the title aloud. "*Willibald Pirckheimer, Albrecht Dürer, and the German Renaissance*, by J. G. San Martin." He flipped a few pages. "J. G. . . . You don't suppose—"

Miles dove for another book. "*Velázquez as Anti-Revolutionary*, by J. G. San Martin. Wasn't he another painter?"

"Seventeenth-century Baroque. We never got around to him. What's that final book?"

"*Spanish Colonial Art in South America*, by J. G. San Martin." Miles set the last book on the floor. "What's going on here, Wick?"

"José has a secret life as a scholar? Who knows? Is there anything else?" Wick felt around the edges of the empty suitcase, as if not believing it was truly empty.

"Wait a minute!" Miles flopped on the tiled floor next to the case.

"What in the world are you doing?"

"Quiet. I'm thinking." He blew away a few dust balls, studied the bottom of the case, partially rose to inspect the empty insides again, then began tapping the sides. "Hear anything?"

"Only the sounds of my brother slowly going insane."

"Come on, Wick. Use your imagination a little. Can't you hear the hollowness on this left side?"

"I never did have much of a musical ear . . . "

Miles ceased tapping and began pressing the inside edges of the case. He was rewarded by a tiny click. The bottom of the suitcase rose before their eyes, revealing a thin sheaf of papers. "Hah! Oh ye of little faith!"

"Move over, Miles."

"Stop grabbing!"

"I'll grab whenever I feel like grabbing!"

Wick snatched the papers and smoothed them out on his lap. "I think it's a report of some sort."

Miles bent over his shoulder. "I can see that! What's it say?"

"You're blocking the light." Miles moved, allowing Wick to study the first page. "The handwriting's a little crabbed. Would you suspect José Gregorio of having a crabbed hand? Small and tight, perhaps, yet stylishly refined—"

"Get on with it, Wick!"

"*Investigations into the Dürerbund*—"

"The Dürerbund?" Miles scratched his head. "That sounds awfully familiar. Wasn't it . . . Yes! The secret society Uncle's art dealer mentioned way back in Paris! Does this mean José has known about it all along?"

In answer, Wick finished reading the title: "—*Being Preliminary Notes by J. G. San Martin on Behalf of Scotland Yard and the Sûreté.*"

"Holy smoke!" breathed Miles. "I *knew* José wasn't a mere servant. He's a spy! Working for the British and French police both! And not letting on for a moment. Now we're getting somewhere!"

✣ ✣ ✣

"I'm hungry!" Miles flung down *Willibald Pirckheimer, Albrecht Dürer, and the German Renaissance.* "José's writing is as heavy as his book. Somehow it's making me hungrier."

"You're the one who couldn't handle dinner. All that nonsense about it being disrespectful to his memory."

"I didn't exactly put it that way. Besides, I don't think José is actually *dead*." He paused thoughtfully. "Maybe in need of rescuing though."

"Why do you think we're studying his collected works? How else will we find any useful clues?"

Miles checked his watch. "It's after eleven. We've been going at this for hours."

"So go downstairs and poke around the kitchen."

"In the dark? In a strange *pensione* in Florence?"

Wick tossed aside the pages he'd been reading. "José certainly takes his time making a point. I suspect he's getting at some ultranationalist business with this Dürerbund."

"What's that mean?" Miles inquired.

"I think the British and French governments are scared this secret society is a front for a new war movement in Germany—using Dürer as a sort of German superman figure to spread nationalistic ideas. The continent's been fairly peaceful for a few decades, and the rest of Europe would like it to continue that way." Wick stretched. "Come on, I'm hungry too."

They crossed the darkened hallway, making for the staircase. "But Dürer wasn't even German!" Miles spat out. "Not according to José's book."

Wick stopped. "What do you mean?"

"Well, only half German. On his mother's side. The side with modest artistic talent. His father, Albrecht the Elder, was a famous Hungarian goldsmith."

"The plot gets more interesting all the time," Wick muttered as they descended the stairs.

They made it to the bottom and headed through the darkened vestibule and dining room toward where they suspected the kitchen lay. Miles bumped into a chair and paused.

"What's the matter?" Wick asked.

"Did you hear something?"

"Only you being clumsy."

"No. Besides me being clumsy."

"Hush. Your imagination's working overtime."

"Is not. Here." Miles purposely jostled another chair. The sound echoed through the empty room. On the edge of the sound, however, was another.

"Footsteps?" Wick was suddenly whispering.

"Definitely," Miles whispered back.

"Headed for the stairs—" Wick stopped cold. "José's manuscript! We left it tossed across my bed!"

"*You* left it—"

"Never mind. Move!"

They raced for the stairs.

Five

"The manuscript's gone!" Wick exclaimed.

"The scoundrels stole Willy Pirckheimer too!" Miles wailed.

"They couldn't have gotten far. They were only a few steps ahead of us—" Wick ran to the hallway to listen for sounds of escape. "Nothing."

Miles dashed for the open window and leaned out. "Forget the hallway, Wick. They took a shortcut. Right out our window."

"What?" Wick joined his brother. Several shadowy figures were rounding the far corner at great speed.

"Skunked!"

In total disgust Wick slammed the window—solidly down on his left hand.

"*Yipes!*"

Miles managed to push it open again.

"Are you all right?"

Wick stuck three inflamed fingers in his mouth. "I'll probably never be able to place another racing bet with this hand." He sank onto the nearest bed. "Did the villains leave us anything?"

"Only the South American and Spanish books. Fat lot of good

they'll do us." Miles chucked them away. "Maybe we should stop racing around like idiots and start using our brains."

"Haven't you heard, brother? We aren't credited with any." Wick absently ran his injured hand through his hair, then flinched. "Fact of the matter is, we're on short credit all around. Lack of brains, lack of common sense, lack of—"

"Well," Miles interrupted, "we've already proven part of that true. We left our evidence just lying here. "

"We weren't expecting any competition for it, were we? Until a few minutes ago I thought this entire José Gregorio business was interesting but far-fetched."

Miles sighed. "It isn't far-fetched anymore. There's a *conspiracy* afoot, and José is in the middle of it. How far did you get with his notes?"

"Nearly all the way through. But there wasn't a lot of information. It sounded more as if he were *trying* to build a case against this Dürerbund but hadn't enough facts to go on."

"What facts did he have?" Miles pressed.

"They're based in Nuremberg, like we thought, because it was Dürer's hometown. Surprisingly, his house is still standing. Nearly four hundred years after he died! His tomb is still intact too, and a heroic statue was raised for him about fifty years back."

"Anything else?" Miles asked.

"Just that there's a huge old guildhall where the bund holds its rituals . . . but its really secret meetings are in some castle tucked away in Bavaria."

"What castle might that be?"

"Never heard of it before. A place called *Schloss Neuschwanstein*."

Miles hauled his leather satchel from beneath his bed.

"What are you doing?"

"Starting to pack. Do you think a couple of fresh shirts and a set of clean underwear will be enough? I don't want to leave behind any of my chemistry kit."

"Packing for where?"

"For Germany, of course. I thought it was obvious, Wick. José's been secretly compiling information on this Dürerbund, hasn't he? And the Dürerbund is based in Germany. Nuremberg, to be exact. Think about it logically. José has disappeared. The only place he could be heading—willingly or unwillingly—is—"

"Germany," Wick deduced. "But that doesn't mean we have to follow him."

Miles glanced up from his labors. "Really, Wick. You wanted to go to Germany anyway, and now José might be on his way there—and might be in serious trouble. Maybe we could help. He *is* the first person who's taken any real interest in us since we outgrew our nanny."

"Sure, lecturing us, just like old Peterson the headmaster."

"But José's lectures are *sincere*, Wick. I think he truly cares about us. Besides, here's your chance to escape!"

"I'd prefer escaping on my own terms," Wick grumbled to himself. But he pulled out his satchel. "All right already. We can always keep a lookout for those *Knot* woodcuts while we're hunting for José." He stopped. "What about Uncle?"

"You heard the doctor. He's so miserable, he doesn't want us anywhere near him."

"He certainly made that obvious enough!"

"So we can leave with clear consciences, Wick. It's not as if we're running away, like we'd been planning. We have a real mission now. You'd better write a note just in case, to cover our tails."

"Why should *I* write the note?"

"You're still the oldest."

Wick frowned as he hunted for paper. "Something to the effect that we'll be carrying on our explorations of various cultural offerings, I suppose?"

"Terrific. It's not even a lie."

"That his good doctor ordered us absolutely *not* to disturb him?" Wick began to scribble. "And that we'll be quiet as mice."

"That's the ticket." Miles stuffed a few maps into his bag. "Oh, and just to be sure he doesn't get the police involved, could we add that José sent a message saying he had to run off on business for a week or so?"

Wick considered. "Brilliant. We'll make it *Uncle's* business. José got a really hot tip on a fabulous masterpiece."

Wick finished the note and shoved it under the door to their uncle's room. Next he headed for his steamer trunk in the corner by the windows. "There's got to be a night train to Germany. Where'd we put that *Baedeker's* four-language dictionary? And the guide-books? I think we're going to need them." He stopped. "Have you been messing with my trunk?"

"Haven't been near it since I helped you haul it to that corner." Miles was trying to cram underwear into his satchel. "Why?"

"I left it open. I distinctly remember that. Now it's closed."

"So? Maybe José was neatening up this morning."

Wick was staring at a short length of rope threaded through one clasp of his trunk. "There's nothing wrong with the locks. Why would José Gregorio tie knots in it?"

"Knots?" Miles hurried over. "That's just one innocent little knot."

"I can see that, Miles. The question is why?"

"For goodness sake, how mysterious can a knot be?" Miles efficiently untied it and tucked the length of rope in his pocket. "There. Now you can open the trunk and get packed."

✛ ✛ ✛

They caught the first northbound train, a 2:00 A.M. local to Genoa. Boarding with a handful of passengers, the boys hurried to their hard third-class benches.

"I don't know why we couldn't at least have sprung for second-class tickets," Wick griped. "Second class has cushions."

"Economy, Wick, economy." Miles scrunched down, pulled up his feet, and gingerly laid his head on his satchel. "At least the carriage is empty and we have these benches to ourselves." He tugged the brim of his straw hat over his eyes.

Wick was flat on his back opposite his brother, knees nearly to his chin. "All very well for you to say. I'm considerably taller." He brushed at a knee. "And whose idea was it to wear our white linens? Mine are already coated with coal dust!"

"No choice." Miles turned away. "José sent off everything else to be cleaned."

A shrill whistle pierced the still night, and the train slowly rolled into it.

✣ ✣ ✣

Shivering in the cool morning air of Genoa's station, Miles prodded Wick.

"Look who's getting out of the first-class compartment of our train!"

Wick stopped patting the wrinkles of his disheveled suit. "Who?"

Miles pulled him behind a pillar. "The tall blond man and the short bald one. Don't they look German?"

Wick shrugged off his brother's arm to peek. "I guess. Don't know that I've seen enough Germans to judge, though, aside from that one in the card game."

"The figures running from our *pensione* last night. It was quite dark; but one was very tall, the other sort of short and squatty. Like them."

"That's not enough evidence to make a connection."

"Just wait. If they board our train to Milan—"

"Milan is hardly Germany, Miles."

"You'll see—"

"*Milano! Milano!*" A conductor strode through the station, bellowing something about track numbers.

"Isn't *Milano* Italian for *Milan*? Come on, Miles. He's announcing our next train."

"Wait." Miles held Wick back. "There! Our Germans are following the conductor! Didn't I tell you? Didn't I say—"

"Grab your bag. If we don't follow him too, we'll miss our bloody connection!"

✣ ✣ ✣

Wick and Miles stumbled around fellow passengers, parcels, and several caged chickens till they found two empty wooden benches. The seats weren't any softer than their earlier ones, but the brothers were too exhausted to complain. They flopped down and slept.

Smells of garlic sausage, cheese, and yeasty bread woke Miles. "Wick!" He kicked his brother. "*Breakfast*." He gaped at the picnickers surrounding them and swallowed. "If only we'd thought to pack some food."

Wick twisted into a sitting position. "We must be getting close to Germany. I could put on a good impression of a pretzel." He shook his legs. "What the dickens is wrong with me now? I feel cramped, almost tied."

Miles stopped salivating over a neighbor's hunk of sausage to study his brother's legs. His eyes widened. "You *are* tied!"

"Don't be ridiculous." Wick craned his neck to inspect his feet. "What in the world?"

"Someone tied your ankles together while we were sleeping! A short length of rope, with two simple knots . . . " Miles groped for his jacket pocket. "It's still here."

Wick rubbed his mussed hair. "What's still there?"

"The other length of rope. The piece that had *one* knot on your trunk."

Leaning over his legs, Wick attacked the knots. They slipped apart with ease. "This is totally ridiculous. Tying a person while he's innocently asleep . . . "

"Not really tying, Wick. Only sort of."

"What's that supposed to mean?"

"It means José didn't make that first knot. *They* did. If they'd really wanted, they could have trussed both of us while we slept. Good and proper. Those were only two little baby knots. Sort of more like a, a . . ."

"Like what? A warning?"

"Well, it's certainly a message." Miles studied their car with new concentration. "We must have been asleep for hours through any number of stops. The chickens are gone, and no one looks the same as when we boarded at Genoa. There's probably no point in even trying to question these people. They're not interested in anything but their breakfasts."

Wick blinked at the sunshine pouring through the grime of their train window. "More like lunch." He thrust the rope into his jacket pocket. "I hope there's a dining car somewhere on this train. Grab your bag and we'll go search for it." He stopped. "And if we pass through first class, look for those two Germans of yours."

✛ ✛ ✛

By evening they were in Zurich, waiting for a train out of Switzerland to Stuttgart, then hopefully on to Nuremberg. They'd never found their Germans on the Milan train but had spotted them boarding the special for Zurich. Once more the suspects had promptly disappeared from sight. Miles had given up trying to locate them in the busy Zurich station and was studying the map of Germany.

"I don't know, Wick. Maybe we should be heading straight for southern Bavaria and that castle you mentioned. It's an awfully long way from Nuremberg back to the mountains again."

"Absolutely not! We've got to reconnoitre the Dürerbund's headquarters first. Besides, there's our original mission to consider too."

"Finding lost art? You're worrying about *art* with José Gregorio in dire danger?"

"We don't know if he's in any danger at all—" Wick broke off to peer into the distance. "Say, those look suspiciously like our two German friends over there."

Miles lowered the map. "Where?"

"Way across the concourse. Stay with the bags. I'll be right back."

Miles stayed with their bags for a full two minutes. Then he impatiently tossed his open map over the cases and ran after his brother.

"Did you find them?" Miles huffed up to Wick.

He nodded. "Over at the café counter. Having cakes. And

coffee with cream. I even saw them add sugar. The blond giant took five cubes."

"That's an awful lot of sugar for such a little cup."

"He's an awfully big man." Wick shook his head, then turned toward his brother. "Where are the bags?"

"Bags?" Miles backed up a step. "I sort of left them where we were, I guess."

"You *left* our bags?"

"It seemed safe enough—"

"Idiot! What if they're stolen?"

"Don't call me an idiot! Besides, if you want to stand here and argue about it all night, they really might get stolen."

Wick spun on his heels and raced back through the terminal. Miles followed, weaving between passengers. When he pulled up short next to his brother, Wick was staring at the map covering the two bags. Miles heaved a sigh of relief. "There. Perfectly safe and sound."

Wick grabbed the opened map. Their bags were still there, but something had been added. This time the short length of rope had been neatly threaded through the handles of Wick's satchel. It was tied with *three* knots.

Miles adjusted his glasses and leaned forward. "Notice how these knots are becoming more intricate, Wick? They're not baby knots anymore. Not to mention that this is the third time it's happened. I'd say there's a definite pattern here. . . . "

Wick was fighting the knots. "These bags," he hissed through gritted teeth, "these bags will never leave our sight again. Not for a moment. Is that clear?" He didn't even wait for Miles's reaction. "And if we sleep on the train tonight, we do it in shifts."

Miles pinched his nose. Finally he spoke. "Both of our Germans were on the other side of the station, guzzling coffee, Wick. While we've been following them, who do you suppose has been following us?"

Six

"**. . . Wurtenberger Hof, conveniently situated near the station;** *Wittelsbacher Hof, Pfannenschmiedsgasse, R.*"

Wick ceased his droning to glance up from *Baedeker's Guide to Southern Germany and Austria* lying open in his lap. "What do you suppose the R stands for? . . . Miles?" He booted his brother curled up on the hard seat across from him.

"What is it? What is it? I'm awake, I truly am . . . "

Wick raised his voice over the clack of the train's iron wheels. "You are not! You promised to help. How am I supposed to stay awake reading this boring list of Nuremberg hotels?"

"Can't afford a proper hotel anyhow," Miles mumbled. "Have to stop at one of these *zimmer* places we've seen advertised near all the little stations."

"But *zimmer* means *room*. It will be like some dreary boarding-house back home."

"You've been spoiled rotten by Uncle's four-star establishments, Wick." Miles rubbed his eyes. "We're not working with the Forrester millions anymore. You might as well get used to the idea." He sat up and straightened his glasses. "Here, give me that book!"

Wick handed it over with a shrug.

"We should read up on the city itself. Its background. How we get around once we're there." Miles thumbed through the Nuremberg section. "This is it."

He began to recite: " 'Nuremberg, population 142,400, a free city of the Empire down to 1806, has since belonged to Bavaria. There is probably no city in Germany still so medieval in appearance . . .' That doesn't tell us much we won't find out when we arrive." He skimmed the page further. "Ah. More to the point.

'Painting was sedulously cultivated as early as the fourteenth century. In order to understand the wide-spread fame of the Nuremberg School, we must keep in mind that printing had recently been invented, engendering a taste for illustrated books, engravings, and woodcuts; the importance of Nuremberg art lies less in the products of the paintbrush than in the humorous and thoughtful creations embodied by means of the burin and the chisel.' " He looked up. "What's a *burin*?"

Wick yawned. "Figure it out. Probably an engraving tool."

"Of course." Miles continued. " 'The characteristic tendency to depth of meaning shows itself in the pictures of Albrecht Dürer (1471—1528), the greatest painter Nuremberg has produced.' That's saying a mouthful, all right. Are you still following me, Wick?"

"Yes, but I'd rather be sleeping. *Baedekers* have a way of doing that to me."

"With a little help from the hour." The book jiggled in his lap as Miles searched for his pocket watch. He snapped it open. "Just after four. And it's still completely black outside. Do you think we'll ever reach Nuremberg? And will we ever get some sleep?"

"Probably yes to both. But not in the immediate future. Have you noticed how long it takes these European trains to get anywhere? At home we could've traveled from New York to California by this time." Wick rolled his neck and arched his back. "More comfortably too. Get on with the Dürer part, Miles."

It took a moment to find his place. "Here we are. 'Nuremberg itself, however, now possesses few products of Dürer's fertile genius;

the only certified examples remaining in his native town are the *Hercules* (an early work), portraits of Emperor Charlemagne—'"Miles stopped again. "How'd you suppose our Albrecht managed that?"

Wick was rubbing his eyes. "Managed what?"

"A portrait of Charlemagne? If Dürer was born in 1471 like it says here, and Charlemagne died about six hundred years earlier . . . "

"You just finished reading about his fertile genius, Miles. He obviously guessed at it and fooled everyone."

"Still, six hundred years—"

"Miles!"

"'. . . his portrait of Emperor Sigismund, and a pieta, all in the Germanic Museum. His best works are to be seen in Vienna, Munich, and Berlin.'" Miles glanced up from the book. "Not a word about his *Knot* series."

"Why should *Baedeker's* single out one little series of six woodcuts when he did all that other, bigger stuff?"

"How do we know it's only six?"

"Because that's what Pierre Polisson said, Miles. And José Gregorio agreed. José said he'd actually seen one a while back. It was a simple woodcut, with a bunch of white lines squiggled across a black background."

"I forgot about that. I guess I wasn't paying much attention at the time."

"Well, we can't go slacking off like at school anymore. You never know when this kind of information might come in handy. Anything else about Dürer?"

But Miles had stopped reading to fumble in his jacket pocket. He pulled out the first length of rope. "Let me see your collection, Wick."

Wick sighed and handed over his two lengths. Miles shoved his glasses to the top of his head and peered closely at the ends.

"Now what are you trying to do?"

"I wish I hadn't had to leave my microscope at the *pensione* in Florence. If it were right here I could prove that these pieces all came from the same coil of hemp. Probably."

"How?"

"By studying a bit of the fiber from the end of each length of rope under the lens. I could even match the cuts. Undoubtedly be able to tell you which piece was snipped first, how—"

"What would all that prove?"

"Oh, I don't know. Just that they all came from the same hand, I suppose."

"We've already guessed that, Miles. What we don't know is *why*. A microscope's never going to tell us that!"

"You really don't have any feeling for science, do you?" Miles tossed the ropes back to his brother. "I'll bet you anything they're connected to Albrecht's *Knot* series though."

"Another genius in our midst. Why don't you tell me something I don't already suspect?"

"I wish I could. . . . But if there are only six woodcuts in the series, what happens after we're presented with the *sixth* knot?"

"We're never going to see a sixth knot. Why do you think we're torturing ourselves staying awake like this? You'd better read some more."

With a scowl Miles soldiered on. "'None of Dürer's pupils developed their activity to any great extent in Nuremberg, however . . .'"

✜ ✜ ✜

Nuremberg's *Bahnhof* was in the modern part of the city. Clutching their satchels and thick bratwurst sandwiches, Wick and Miles staggered from the station into the twilight. They booked a room in the first *zimmer* they could find. Safely inside, they locked the windows, barricaded the door with the room's only chair, finished their meal, and toppled into the lone bed, dead to the world.

They woke when Wick thrashed past his half of the bed, propelling Miles over the side with a thump.

"What's that sound?" Wick shot from under the covers. "Is someone at the door?"

"No. I'm on the floor."

Wick leaned over the edge of the mattress. "So you are. What are you doing down there?"

Miles stood up and brushed at his bare legs. "I was on the floor because you pushed me there, Wick."

"Oh."

Miles squinted down. "An amazingly clean floor too. Not a speck of dust. Signora Bellini could take a few lessons from our new landlady."

Wick got out of bed, covering his knees with his shirttails. He swept the nearest curtain aside and cracked open a window. "Aah . . ." He breathed in deeply. "I think we survived. It would appear to be morning already." He scratched at a knobby knee. "I do miss my pajamas though."

Miles started prowling around the small room. "All windows intact. Chair still shoved under the doorknob." He reached for the glasses he'd left perched on the tiny washstand and hooked them over his ears. Then he stooped to inspect their bags. "Nary a knot in sight."

"Good sign. Excellent sign." Wick stepped into his wrinkled trousers and poured water from a pitcher into the washbasin. "Cute. Little forget-me-nots painted all over the bowl to cheer my day." He splashed his face, wet a comb, and pulled it through his hair. "A good night's sleep was all we needed, Miles. Add a hearty breakfast, and Nuremberg will be ours!"

"We should probably start by getting the lay of the land. You know, walking around the ramparts of the old city, checking out its towers." Miles pulled on his trousers and tucked in his shirt. "I'm really looking forward to examining the moat. It's dry now, but I've never seen a proper moat. And this one's said to be thirty-five yards wide and thirty-three feet deep. That should be fairly impressive."

"I say we head directly to the Dürer Platz and our boy's house." Wick shrugged into his jacket. "This isn't supposed to be a sightseeing trip, after all. We're on a mission." He grinned. "You remember Uncle Eustace that first night aboard ship? All that stuff about organizing battle strategies? And how we were invading Europe? How little he knew!"

"And there was José Gregorio, masterfully handing Uncle his glass of bromide." Miles smiled appreciatively. "José could certainly act!"

"Let's hope our valet's still keeping up the role." Wick tugged the heavy chair away from the door and rested one hand on the knob. "You ready?"

Miles clapped his straw boater on his head. "Sure. But we have to walk past a lot of interesting stuff anyhow, and I don't understand why we can't take a few minutes to inspect it. There's the Industrial Museum which could have some very useful scientific models. . . . What's the matter now?"

Wick had opened the door and was staring at the outside knob with an expression akin to fear and loathing.

"Tell me it's not another—"

"*Four* knots! Count them! Four knots looped around the knob like some kind of a—" Wick's voice broke.

Miles patted his brother's shoulder. "It's all right. We mustn't let these warnings get to us. We'd be playing right into their hands . . . whoever *they* might be. José's Dürerbund, probably. Nobody else would use Albrecht's art as a symbol. And anyway, this is nowhere near to a noose knot." He knelt to inspect the configurations more closely. "Quite interesting, actually. These are closer to something I read about once. I think they're called Turk's head knots. See how they look like little turbans? That must be really hard to do."

Wick grabbed Miles and jerked him up. "You are *not* supposed to be admiring these people!"

"But a job well done in any endeavor—"

"Miles, Miles." Wick's grip tightened almost painfully.

"Yes?"

He let go. "Get rid of that thing!"

"You needn't shout." Miles carefully rearranged his jacket. "Do you mind if I don't destroy the knot this time? I'd like to study it, see if I could make one of these myself."

Wick stamped down the hall. "I'll be outside. Don't bother locking anything. What's the point? What's the point of this entire exercise?"

"I did lock up." Miles joined his brother, who'd already stalked halfway down the street. "And I took the precaution of leaving my bag with Frau Hellman for safekeeping. Also, I remembered our *Baedeker.*"

Wick was still furious, still had his fists balled tightly in his pockets. "You needn't have taken the trouble."

"You're being defeatist, Wick. Playing straight into the opposition's hands. Have these people actually done anything nasty to us? No. They just keep leaving their calling cards."

"Upping the ante each time. Never forget that!"

Miles skipped to keep up with his brother's longer strides. "Well, you're a gambler, aren't you? If you were to think of it as a card game, or a really close horse race . . . "

They'd wandered north in the direction of the old city from their little rooming house. Wick strode forward in silence for a few blocks, then crossed a wide, modern street to face the moat. Miles hung back to sightsee as his brother plowed through medieval gates and entered the ancient walled city. After another few blocks Wick halted by the Pegnitz River. When Miles caught up, Wick pulled his hands from his pockets and stretched the tension from his fingers.

"You may be right, Miles. If this is a game, then maybe what's called for is total focus. Total concentration."

Miles breathed a sigh of relief. "That's more like it. And besides, you always win at games."

Wick stared across the river. "Practically always."

⁜ ⁜ ⁜

They crossed the Pegnitz through an old covered bridge and headed deeper into the warren of ancient buildings: houses leaning drunkenly into each other; thatched roofs overlapping slate; stucco crumbling from half-timber walls. The streets were as crooked as the houses. After negotiating a few sudden, illogical turns, Miles began dallying by the corners of buildings, poking his nose around them.

"You can cut out the cloak-and-dagger stuff, Miles," called Wick. "These old buildings have millions of hiding places. We'll know if the Dürerbund's following us when they're good and ready to show themselves."

Miles edged away from another corner in mild disappointment. "You really think so?"

"I've been working it out while we walked. There's no place at all for *us* to hide. We might as well just go about our business."

"But—"

"Look." Wick waited for Miles to catch up, then pointed toward a nearby sloping roof. "What does that tiny oval window in the roof remind you of?"

"Now that you mention it, well . . . an *eye*."

"In case you hadn't noticed, they're all over the roofs. *Eyes*."

Miles shivered. "I wish you hadn't made that little observation. Now I feel as if *everything's* staring at us."

"Precisely."

Wick walked on. He didn't stop till the warren of streets opened onto a square near the foot of massive fortifications. "That must be Nuremberg's castle, the Kaiserburg, up there." He nodded. "I think we've arrived."

"Dürer Platz? How do you know?" Miles lowered his eyes from the ramparts. "Oh."

A statue of heroic dimensions stood in the center of the square, its back facing them. Miles darted in front of a milk wagon to reach it. Wick got caught on the far side by a hearse leading a cortège of carriages. The funeral procession took its time winding its mournful way across the plaza. As it disappeared into the streets beyond, Wick crossed the square to join his brother.

"Nothing like another omen to improve one's morning. So how is Albrecht today?" He rounded the statue to inspect the face. "He's aged since we last met. . . . *Son of a gun.* Now he really does look—"

"Like Christ?" Miles suggested. "Those locks flowing down to his shoulders, the noble face—not to mention the beard. Maybe a little older though, as if Christ had lived another ten years and wore an ermine collar on his robes."

"*Wow!*" Wick circled the statue a few more times. "Someone's certainly made our Albrecht monumental. If this is how the Dürerbund thinks of him . . . Well, it's almost enough to make you understand why they've developed a cult around the man."

Miles stood back to take in the entire memorial, pedestal and all. "I'll bet there's not a single statue of an artist in the entire United States of America, Wick. Only dead presidents and Civil War generals. And mostly they're boring. Take Grant's Tomb—"

"I don't want Grant's Tomb, Miles. I wouldn't mind taking Albrecht home though. Can't you see him hulking over Mother's garden?"

"Why, that's it! I *knew* there was something familiar. He's as formidable as Mother!"

"Mother doesn't wear a full beard."

"Not yet . . . "

Wick swatted his brother. "Enough of that. It's time to move on to Dürer's house." He slowly pivoted, taking in the entire square, then gestured toward the north. "It ought to be a block or two in that direction, if the map can be trusted. Come on." Wick set off at a clip as Miles puffed to keep up.

"Are we there yet? How will you know when—" Miles stopped.

"That building on the far corner, facing us." Wick halted at the base of the Kaiserburg. "It's got to be. See the little medallion over the front door?"

"Not bad!" Miles whistled as he studied the substantial house, its walls half-timber above several stories of stone. "It must have six floors, if you count that space under the slanted roof. And it's solid, just like Dürer." He smiled. "I'm glad to see he wasn't a starving artist but made a few bucks in his time. It's sort of comforting. How do we get in?"

"How soon you forget your *Baedeker*." Wick started across the open plaza below the castle. "It's run by a society. We knock."

❖   ❖   ❖

Wick banged on the massive wooden doors set on the edge of the sloping, cobbled street. The boys waited. Wick pounded some more.

In due time a tiny door set within the larger ones rasped open. Red-rimmed, watery eyes peered out at them.

"*Ja? Was ist?*"

"*Ist* tourists. May we enter?"

The little door slammed. Miles glanced at Wick. "Is he going to let us in?"

"I'm not sure. . . . "

Creeeeaak.

Protesting mightily, the portals spread wide. A gnomelike creature, hunched almost in half, greeted them.

"*Die Engländer?*"

"*Nein.* American."

"*Willkommen.*" The keeper pointed toward a staircase, then hobbled to a rear window behind the stairs, where sunlight shone on a worktable.

Wick ventured over the threshold. "I guess we're allowed to just walk around."

"Wait a minute, Wick. I'd like to see what he's working on."

Miles followed the old man, who'd settled into a hard chair and was reaching for a brush. With surprisingly steady fingers he began painting a sheet of stained glass.

"Lovely," Miles breathed. "Come see, Wick. He's drawing pictures on colored glass, just like the windows in Notre Dame in Paris. Only it's not saints he's making. It looks more like some kind of a maze."

The old man glanced up from his labors. "*Irrgarten. Labyrinth.*"

Wick hovered over the work. "What a queer thing to put on stained glass."

"It's only a small piece of glass. Probably for a small window. And the labyrinth's quite fine. You could almost walk through it in your mind. I especially like the center."

Wick leaned closer. "That's another queer thing. Whoever heard of a rabbit in the center of a labyrinth?"

The old man smiled. "*Hase. Dürer's Hase.*"

Wick bit his lip. "Wait a minute. It's coming back. Two years of struggling over German at school. But just to be sure . . . " He pulled a dictionary from his pocket and flipped through it. "Yes! *Hase* is *Hare*." He beamed at the old man. "*Gut!*"

The old man beamed back, then bent over his work. Miles tugged at his brother's sleeve. "He wants privacy. Let's get on with exploring the house."

✣ ✣ ✣

There was a lot of bulky old furniture, heavy drapes and rugs, and poor copies of Dürer works hanging on the walls. Miles was briefly distracted by an indoor kitchen with a vast beehive oven. But when he caught sight of a familiar image in a bedroom under the eaves at the top of the house, he got really excited. "Take a look at this, Wick."

"What is it?" Wick wandered over. "Oh, another copy."

"But it's the rabbit, Wick! Don't you see? The same one the old man was copying onto glass downstairs." He lifted his glasses to squint at the image. "It says 1502, and there's Albrecht's signature—the little *D* lodged under the fancy, great *A*, as if it's hiding beneath a tabletop, squinched between the two legs of the *A*."

"So what, Miles?"

"Now you're the one with the short memory. How could you forget Uncle dragging us off on that day trip to Chartres Cathedral? Don't you remember the labyrinth inlaid on the floor in the west end of the nave?"

"Well, it was fairly worn out. . . . "

"But José Gregorio said it was special. In the Middle Ages pilgrims used to travel there. They'd get down on their hands and knees and crawl around the whole thing."

"Now it comes back." Wick brushed at his graying white trousers. "How any human being could lower himself to that extent—"

"But José said the maze was a symbol, Wick, for people getting lost in life's labyrinthine ways. Each dead end stood for a sin. When you finally made it to the center, that meant you'd overcome everything—all the temptations."

"What kind of temptations could those poor sods have had in the Middle Ages?" Wick asked. "Think of the way they lived. All that nasty serfdom, and tobacco hadn't even been discovered!"

"They had devils, too, Wick. They must have. Why else would there be gargoyles all over their cathedrals? And anyway, you're missing the main point."

"What point?"

"The middle of the maze! Good grief, Wick, *think*. Crawling to the center of the maze meant you'd made it to the ultimate!"

Wick considered. "I guess José did mention something about the center being considered Jerusalem. And after suffering through all those Crusades, Jerusalem meant heaven—or God. That would suggest—"

"*Yes. Yes!*" Miles was having a hard time restraining his enthusiasm. "Maybe the old man's a part of the Dürerbund! The rabbit—"

"Hare."

"Hare, whatever. I never did catch the distinction—"

"But you're the one so big on scientific precision. Doesn't a hare have longer legs or something?"

Miles tried to calm himself. "I'll ask Father in my next letter. Really, Wick. I thought you were going to *focus*. Don't you see that this, this *animal* . . . Maybe—just maybe—it stands for Dürer? He's been placed in the holiest of holies, the center of the *maze*."

"Connecting our Albrecht directly to God—or at least something pretty darn close, like a saint or something."

"*Finally.*"

"This obviously requires further thought."

Wick's stomach growled. "Since we've already missed breakfast, I suggest we proceed to lunch. And maybe a stein of beer. If we want to think like Germans, we ought to emulate their behavior."

Seven

"Ugh!"

Miles reacted emphatically to his first taste of beer. He spat the mouthful onto the floor of the *biergarten*, wiping the remaining mustache of foam on his sleeve.

"Really, Miles. You've probably insulted the entire fatherland. All the waiters are staring at you." Wick savored a frothy sip from his own stein.

"Don't care. Give me a nice glass of wine any day."

Wick shrugged. "We're not in France anymore."

"In fact, you could even give me a glass of milk. It would taste good about now."

"Milk doesn't go with sausage and sauerkraut."

Miles took up his fork and cleared every strand of sauerkraut from his sausage before slicing into it. "Don't like cabbage either. Never have." He tested a bite. "Germans do make a nice sausage though. Hearty."

Wick reached for his brother's stein of beer and lined it up next to his own. "Waste not, want not."

"Bad idea, Wick." Miles swallowed. "We're supposed to be concentrating. And how can you concentrate if you drink all that beer? Somehow it seems more lethal than wine. Maybe I ought to be doing another alcohol content analysis—"

"Excuse me, gentlemen."

"We didn't order anything else, thank you." Miles glanced up. It wasn't their waiter. It was, in fact— "Pierre Polisson!"

"In the flesh." The art dealer swept off his cape, draped it over an extra chair, and sat. "What a delightful surprise to encounter known faces among strangers. Especially as I was under the impression that the Forrester party was currently basking in the heat of more southerly climes. I trust I may join you?" He snapped a finger and a waiter was instantly by his side.

"*Mein Herr?*"

"*Bier. Und. . .*" He waved toward Miles's plate of sausage. The waiter got the message and dashed off.

Wick eyed his two steins of beer regretfully. Obviously his consumption had just been curtailed. "We did Italy rather quickly . . ."

"How is dear Mr. Forrester?" Polisson blithely ran over Wick's words. "Shall I expect him to be joining us shortly?"

"No," Miles piped up. "He stayed in—"

"—the hotel." Wick cut off his brother's words while giving him a sharp kick under the table. "Resting up after our journey. The Wurtenberger Hof," he dredged up from memory.

"A pity, I'm at the *Wittelsbacher Hof* myself. It might have been pleasant to meet with him." Polisson stroked his goatee. "But I could always visit."

"Uncle's really quite worn out." Miles rubbed his leg but played along with the deception. "José Gregorio's drawing his bath. Uncle soaks for hours sometimes. And then José will do his massage . . ."

"Quite a find that valet, isn't he?"

Wick was beginning to adjust to Polisson's unexpected

appearance. He boldly sipped at his beer. "A man among servants. A gem."

"A pearl," Miles added unnecessarily, after which they all stared at one another.

"So," Wick finally broke the silence. "What brings you to Nuremberg, Monsieur Polisson?"

"Business." Polisson smiled as his order arrived. "And you really can't get a decent glass of beer in Paris."

The art dealer addressed his drink and food, then began to chatter about a few new pieces Uncle Eustace might like. Finally, he wiped his mouth and rose. "I believe you'll be returning home through Paris? And that I can expect another visit from your estimable guardian?" Without waiting for an answer, Polisson uttered a cheerful "*Wiedersehen,*" and disappeared.

Miles made a face at his congealed sausage. "Maybe you were right to put Pierre off about Uncle Eustace. It's probably better he doesn't know we're here on our own. I don't trust him. He was the first one to mention the Dürerbund, after all. What do you suppose his little visit was about, anyhow?"

Before his brother could answer, their waiter presented the bill. Wick studied it.

"It was about that stinker putting his lunch on our tab!"

He slapped the chit on the table to return to his beer but gave up on that too. "It's gone flat."

✜ ✜ ✜

"I think we checked every old print dealer in town. None of them knew anything about the Dürerbund. None of them ever heard of Dürer's *Knots.*" Miles and Wick were walking back to their room, weary after their fruitless afternoon tramping around Nuremberg.

"Do you think it was mostly the language problem?" Wick asked.

Miles shook his head. "They knew who Albrecht was right enough. Not that we could have afforded to buy one of their prints anyway. How much money do you suppose we've got left, Wick?"

"Hardly enough. We had to pay Frau Hellman up front for three nights. And after all those train fares, and luncheon today . . . "

"Right. Now we've really got something to dislike about Polisson. Taking advantage of us the way he did."

Wick scowled in remembrance. "Then there was that tip we gave Dürer's hunchback this morning."

"It's the expected thing to do, Wick."

They entered their rooming house and nodded at Frau Hellman stationed behind her little counter as they made for the stairs. She motioned for them to wait while she stooped to retrieve Miles's bag.

"*Danke schön.* I almost forgot about this." Miles grabbed it and continued up the stairs in front of his brother. "I just wish we could have found a clue about the guildhall, or whatever you call it, where the bund's supposed to have their meetings. Since Dürer is the only lead we've got to tracking down José . . . " He glanced down the hallway toward their room. "Hey, wait a minute! Stop!"

Wick mounted the last stair behind him. "What are you yelling about?" Then he saw the startled figure by their room—and something hanging from their doorknob. "Forget the knot, Miles! Catch the villain!"

It wasn't really a matter of chasing him. There was only one exit to the floor, and Wick was blocking it. Miles tried swatting the man with his satchel, but his swing missed by inches. The intruder barreled past—knocking off Miles's straw hat—and shoved Wick aside, taking three steps at a time in his rush for the ground floor and escape.

"This way, Miles!" Still reeling, Wick leaped after him.

✢ ✢ ✢

They'd managed to keep the figure in sight clear across the city until they reached the old walled town. Shadows were falling over buildings as the sun dropped behind the rooftops. In a matter of moments night fell. Darkness surrounded them.

"Blast it! He's disappeared into this rabbit's warren." Wick stopped for breath. "We've lost him!"

Miles leaned against a wall, clutching his satchel and gasping. Bits of crumbling stucco fell onto his head. "The whole city is disintegrating, along with us. And I left my boater back on Frau Hellman's floor." He brushed the debris from his hair. "There's something to be said for America, Wick. Solid. New."

"You don't have to sell me, brother. I never wanted to leave it. Now that we're four thousand miles or so away though . . ."

Wick jammed himself against the same wall as a carriage rattled along the narrow, cobblestoned street. It came so close that he had to draw himself up very straight and thin to miss being crushed.

"Phew! Traveling without lights. That's downright treacherous. You'd think they'd have a law against it."

Miles grabbed him. "Into this doorway, quick! Another's coming!"

They just made safe harbor as the second carriage passed. This one was open, and even in the dark the boys could see the four figures seated inside.

"Look at that, Wick!" Miles whispered. "They're wearing the strangest clothing. I know it's a cool evening for early July, but robes and cloaks? Funny hats?"

"Almost medieval," Wick murmured. As a third closed carriage followed, he grabbed Miles. "Yes. Pay dirt, little brother!"

"What'd you mean?"

"What day is it?"

"How should I know what day it is? They're all jumbled together in my head."

"Think. It's got to be Saturday. A fine night for a lodge meeting—just like the Moose or Elks back home."

"So?"

"So that last carriage—that very fine barouche—just happened to have a certain young hare painted in gold on its door, like a coat of arms."

"You mean—"

"Right! Who else but the Dürerbund could have such a passion for rabbits? *And* Albrecht-style costumes? We've got to follow these carriages."

"How?"

"Quiet. Here comes the end of the procession. An opera bus with its shades drawn. Perfect. Watch me."

Wick waited for the clatter of iron-shod hooves against stone to pass, then jumped out behind the large coach. Racing after it, he timed himself to the vehicle's bounces. Grasping a protruding rim beneath the closed windows, he used it as a lever to hoist himself onto the rear step.

Miles was having a harder time catching up, burdened as he was by his satchel. Wick stretched out a hand to him. The first try landed them both back on the street's hard cobbles. For once Wick didn't complain—only picked himself up, trotted after the coach, and tried again. Soon they were both precariously perched.

"Wouldn't it have been easier just to chase after it, Wick?" Miles whispered.

"Hush. They would've heard us. Got a decent grip? Hold on!"

✤ ✤ ✤

The convoy of carriages passed through more darkened streets and across the Dürer Platz, then wound its way up to the fortress the boys had seen earlier that day. The vehicles went under an arch, then stopped to discharge passengers. Wick nudged Miles, and they jumped off. Slinking behind the courtyard's lone tree, they watched as the costumed characters gathered to solemnly march toward the castle itself.

"They're heading for that tower to the far side," Wick murmured. "Now they're all inside. . . . The last carriage has disappeared downhill. Let's go."

The huge door to the tower was slightly ajar. Wick forced it farther open, to the screech of ancient hinges.

"Ow." Miles rubbed his ears. "Someone's bound to have heard that."

Wick poked his head inside. "No one around to hear it." He paused to listen to the lingering echoes of footsteps. "They've gone *down* rather than *up* the stairs. Come on."

"Wick?" Miles followed him into the entryway lit by torches on either side of the door. He dropped his bag and adjusted his eyes to the flickering light. It illuminated curious iron implements decorating the walls. "Um . . . Any idea what these might be? They look really old, yet they're polished as if they could be used right this minute."

Wick studied the objects. "Those two"—he pointed—"are manacles of some kind. Leg irons?" He turned. "The handles with chains and spiky stars at their ends, well, I hate to think what they'd have been used for."

"Implements of punishment, Wick." Out of one eye Miles glimpsed an object tucked into a corner. "And what in the world is that? It looks like some sort of a press. But surely not for grapes, not with that round, empty iron cap beneath the screw, just waiting for . . . "

Wick approached the thing and gave the screw a turn. It moved surprisingly smoothly. "A head," he choked. "It's a skull crusher. We've stumbled onto a torture chamber here, Miles. Let's move right along."

Miles scampered for the door with alacrity. "That's fine and dandy with me!"

Wick dragged him back. "Not out, Miles. *Down.*"

"I don't *want* to go down. Who knows what other abominations are hidden there? All oiled and ready to use!"

Wick propelled his brother toward the carved stone steps winding down into blackness. "Nevertheless, you wanted a clue and here it is. Think about poor José Gregorio. He may be down there."

Miles dug in his heels. "He's way older than we are, Wick. He's already lived a full life. Why, if I got to be his age—forty or so—I'd consider myself lucky. In fact, if I live another day or two, I'll consider myself lucky—"

"Stop blathering, Miles."

"I'm not blathering. Just looking at the situation realistically."

"I'm going below. And I'm not going alone."

Miles refused to budge. "A dungeon is what's waiting down there. Couldn't be anything else . . . A dungeon with dried-out skeletons, and maybe a few fresher ones. This is above and beyond the call of duty!"

A sudden, deafening blast of sound surged up the steps to meet them.

Miles lost his balance and thudded onto the clammy floor. "What's that?"

"The tolling of hell's bells reaching up for us." Wick extended a hand to his brother. "Pull yourself together. It's only an organ playing Wagner. *The Ride of the Valkyries* from *Siegfried*, I'm pretty sure. How could you forget that opera we were forced to attend with Mother over Christmas holidays?" He tugged at Miles. "A bunch of silly old guys dressed up in costumes and listening to Richard Wagner—how wicked could they be?"

Miles surrendered. He snatched his bag and followed his brother into the unknown, protesting under his breath the entire way.

Eight

The steps spiraled into the earth forever. Wick and Miles hugged the roughly hewn stone of the staircase well, feeling for each foothold. After rounding many turns, a sputtering torch that jutted from a rough iron bracket surprised them with light. Wick sprang from the wall to rub his jacket sleeve.

"*Yuck.* I'm all green and slimy from mold!"

Miles grabbed his brother's other arm. "Forget about being elegant for once and give me a hand with my satchel."

Wick noticed it for the first time. "Why on earth have you lugged it clear across town?"

"Well, I didn't know we'd be coming clear across town, did I? And I couldn't very well just drop it by the door to our room. Events sort of precipitated things. Hey, watch how you swing that! Here, just give it back." Miles caught the bag. "Watch where you put your feet too! These steps are dangerous, all hollowed out. Probably by eons worth of prisoners being cast into the dungeons, never to return."

"Stop dramatizing, Miles. It would take millions of prisoners to make these dents."

"Well, then, *millions* of poor, innocent souls being led to their doom in tears and lamentation!"

"Jailers probably wore down the steps too." Wick began getting into the spirit of the place. "Taking food below—"

"There'd be no food, nor drink either. The captives would have to lick moisture from these scummy walls and catch vermin for sustenance." Miles paused. "The music's getting louder, Wick."

"Building to a crescendo. We'd better hurry while it still drowns our footsteps!"

The two picked up speed, then slowed at the bottom of a final turn. A torch-lit corridor opened before them, with another leading to the right.

"Which way do we go?"

Wick considered. "The music seems to be coming from straight ahead. We wouldn't want to storm into the middle of things. Let's try the right path."

They crept along the shadowy passageway until it made a left turn, dead-ending into a small, open gallery. Wick dropped to his knees, dragging Miles with him. They crawled toward the front of the narrow balcony. Both aimed for the first opening between stone balusters. They cracked skulls. Miles pulled back, rubbing his head.

"Ow!" he whimpered. "That smarts!"

"Shut up," Wick hissed. "Move over and let's see what's going on."

Finally settled, they examined the scene.

"Gosh!" The last organ notes echoing and reechoing through the space covered Miles's exclamation.

Before them lay a vast, natural cavern half as big as a football field. An enormous set of organ pipes curtained the far wall, the instrument's console looming like an altar. As the boys watched, the organist rose from his seat. Garbed in flowing robes with a cowl hiding his features, he faced the gathering while a small, hunched figure scuttled up to his side. The acolyte raised his arm, solemnly offering a sword. The musician took it, holding it horizontally in front of his body, as if displaying a precious reliquary. The long blade sparkled in the light thrown by rows of enormous candles blazing on either side. The organist, now transformed into a high priest, looked out over his flock, which was waiting in hushed expectancy.

In the moment of silence, the boys saw the island of mosaics stretching across the floor, separating congregation from priest.

"Son of a gun!" Wick's mouth fell open. "There's a giant labyrinth on the floor!"

"Ssh," Miles warned. He studied the rest of the great space. The walls on either side were equally fascinating. The rough rock had been smoothed, plastered, and decorated with frescoes. Unlike the frescoes in Florence, these didn't show a single saint or mythological god. Instead, the set of three huge images on either wall portrayed white lines etched against black backgrounds. The lines squiggled and turned into curlicues and arabesques. Each of the six designs had subtle differences, yet they all culminated in an open center—some with black circles but most with medallions of white.

"Knots!" Miles murmured. "Dürer's *six Knots!*"

Wick gestured toward the mosaic decorating the floor. It was more ornate than the other six. And its center medallion held an image—the image of a young hare. Wick didn't need to say anything. The brothers stared into each other's eyes. Their lips formed the silent words:

"*The seventh Knot!*"

✛ ✛ ✛

A ringing cry from the celebrant drew them back to the ongoing spectacle. His right fist gripped the hilt of the gleaming sword. He swung it out, then up. The motion caused his cowl to slip, revealing stern, hatchet-sharp cheekbones, graying blond hair, and a fierce, beaklike nose.

"He looks an awful lot like that German giant from the train, Wick—"

"But he's not the same person. This man's much older. His small helper though . . ." Wick stared across the distance with amazement. "Could it be?"

Miles could hardly help making the connection. "It's Dürer's hunchback! The keeper of his house!"

"*Heil, Dürer!*" the celebrant screamed.

"*Heil, Dürer!*" his devotees roared back.

The boys' eyes widened in disbelief.

"*Heil, Vaterland!*"

"*Heil*—"

"*Heil*, this is becoming monotonous. This is—" Wick's complaint was choked by a hand gripping him by the scruff of his neck. A second hand reached for Miles.

"What have we here? Two small American rats?"

The voice was harsh. Guttural. "Two small American rats come to spy on the Dürerbund in its most secret guildhall? Its holy sanctuary?"

Miles twisted his neck and squinted into the shadows behind. "*You're* the blond giant! From Florence, and the train! Who are you?"

"Erik von Klein." The figure made a mocking bow. "At your service."

"Charmed, I'm sure," Wick drawled, swatting at the fingers still clutching his neck. For his efforts he was shaken again.

"We meet face-to-face at last," the giant continued. "In time for me to explain the proceedings led by my father. Listen well, and learn. It might enlighten your dim, young minds."

Wick tried to free himself. "I resent that! I've been following the German just fine!"

"All three words of it. My compliments." Von Klein loosened his grip. "Watch. Why not? Never will you survive to report these sacred ceremonies."

Miles didn't care for the implications of that statement. "We have an uncle waiting nearby," he bluffed. "Uncle Eustace is a famous man, a very rich man. He won't tolerate your barbaric treatment of us."

"Shut your mouth! Our *Führer*, our leader, my father—the estimable Graf Otto von Klein—is about to speak!"

He was. And he did, with the passion of one possessed. The demagoguery was broken only by Erik's reverent translation.

"Graf Otto speaks of the most righteous Albrecht Dürer's genius. A man before his time, teaching Germans of their traditions, their greatness; leaving us mysteries to pursue. . . . Now the graf moves on to more modern times, keeping Dürer always before us as a guiding light, since our current German government has not the foresight to do so. He expounds on the necessity of gathering strength, gathering arms, making ready for the culmination of Dürer's goals—the expansion of German brilliance and Empire over all of Europe! Over all the world!"

Wick was not impressed. "Isn't your father pushing this Saint Dürer business over the edge? He was an artist, after all, barely interested in religion or politics—"

"*Infidel!*" Von Klein spat in Wick's face.

Wick swiped at the spittle. "All right, so in Dürer's name, the graf's going to upset your rightful government? Conquer Germany and the world with a few swords and a handful of old men?"

Once more Erik's fingers tightened around Wick's neck. "Do not speak of what you will never understand. On land, over the sea, even in the air we will be supreme!"

Miles snickered. "In the *air*? Are these guys planning to sprout wings? There's been no scientific proof of the possibility of *proper* air flight. Only the romances of fantasy writers like Jules Verne—"

He was rewarded with a sharp cuff to one ear. "Silence! It is happening as we speak. As for these men, they are the local leaders of the movement, chosen from all of Bavaria. Even greater gatherings will take place. The cabal is growing. At the grand leadership meeting next week—"

"In Neuschwanstein?" Miles asked, rubbing his throbbing ear.

"How do you know of *Schloss Neuschwanstein?* How *could* you know?"

Miles clapped hands over both ears but was saved by something stirring in the cavern below. The waiting congregation was forming a long line that slowly, ceremoniously slithered—snake-like—to the entry point of the seventh knot.

"The sacred ceremony," Erik murmured. "On the most sacred of labyrinths—Dürer's final and most secret knot. Oh, that I had been chosen worthy of the honor! My father must see, must understand that I am ready!"

One by one the figures prostrated themselves on the floor and began crawling on hands and knees through the maze. Wick and Miles watched in amazement as the ritual continued in perfect silence. When each votary reached the center he kissed the rabbit, then waited to be raised by the touch of Graf Otto von Klein's sword.

"Boy, this is the dumbest thing I've ever seen," Miles protested. "Our Albrecht would've been annoyed too. He wasn't political and he wasn't stupid. He wasn't even German!"

"*Heathen!*" cried Erik. "Guard closely what comes from your lips!"

"My brother's right, von Klein." Wick rushed to Miles's defense. "Surely you know Dürer is a Hungarian name, from the southeast, near Transylvania. I looked it up on our maps—"

"Enough! I have heard enough! Such blasphemies cannot, *will not*, be countenanced! You will rue the moment you chose to ignore the knotted warnings of my associates."

Erik von Klein's fists tightened with passion. "Now it is time to offer you to the tender mercies of my father. It is only by chance I was assigned guard duty in this sector. Our leader will understand that as a predetermined event, however. If he will not honor me with full membership in the bund at last, at least he will allow me to mete out your punishment."

Wick struggled to his feet with as much aplomb as possible. "Chin up, Miles. It'll take more than Erik and the entire Dürerbund to get the best of the Forrester brothers!"

Miles lifted his chin—and his satchel—and fell in place before the giant.

✣ ✣ ✣

Wick had spoken in a vainglorious attempt to improve morale. He began to pray his words were true as Erik von Klein propelled them into the cavern amid the pomp and ceremony. As their presence was noted, a curious thing happened. An unnerving hiss spread throughout the vast room. Bund members pulled themselves into their robes and cowled their heads from sight as a turtle might pull within its shell at the sign of danger.

The boys feigned nonchalance as they climbed over the bodies wriggling through the labyrinth, while Graf Otto von Klein stood aloof. When they arrived before the leader at last, he raised his sword threateningly—but not toward Wick and Miles. Instead, Erik bore the brunt of the graf's wrath.

"*Dummkopf! Was ist?*"

"*Vater*—"

Wick cherished a brief hope that the graf's sword might eliminate Erik's misery forever. Unfortunately, von Klein lowered the weapon. Harsh language sped between father and son. Too soon, Wick and Miles found themselves being roughly dragged off—this time toward an irregular arch set between two of Dürer's wall knots.

✣ ✣ ✣

Erik von Klein led the way with a torch, followed by Miles, clinging to his bag, then Wick, and finally the old hunchback. As the sights and sounds of the great cavern faded behind them, the small group navigated another endless black passageway.

Erik bent beneath the lowering ceiling of bedrock and stopped at last. The boys found themselves facing a formidable, iron-banded oaken door set within a stone wall. Erik produced a huge key and inserted it in the ancient lock. With much creaking and groaning, the door swung open. Von Klein shoved Wick through but held Miles back.

"Your bag!" he ordered.

"No!"

Erik grabbed for it and Miles stubbornly hung on.

The hunchback limped up and deftly broke the tug-of-war. Von Klein snarled. The hunchback murmured something in the giant's ear.

"What does it matter?" Erik growled. "Nothing will help you now!" He pushed Miles and his bag after his brother. The door clanked shut and the key turned. Definitively. Only the hunchback lingered on the far side of the barrier.

"*Amerikanern*," he whispered through a tiny open grating. "It is with grief I seal you in your death chamber. Few admire my work or leave a gift for old Hans. God speed you to a quick end."

Two sets of footsteps echoed through the passageway, one a driven staccato, the other a tentative shuffle. Along with the footsteps all light disappeared. Miles set down his hard-won satchel.

"Well. It seems as if I was right after all, Wick. There *are* dungeons down here, and we're getting to inspect them firsthand. Although if old Hans is so upset about the situation, you'd think he'd do more than wish us a quick end." Miles grinned through the darkness. "Then again, that tip we gave him did save my bag!"

Wick's shrug was lost in the gloom. "I don't know about you, Miles, but I have no intention of licking any water from scummy walls, or dining on vermin—" A slight noise stopped him. "Did you hear something? Something over in that far corner?"

Miles grabbed his brother. "What do you mean by *something*, Wick?"

"How should I know? Mice? Giant man-eating spiders? What sort of creatures could live down here in this murk, after all? Blast but it's dark! Wait till I find a match . . . " Wick shook off Miles to fumble with an inside jacket pocket and pull out a crumbling cigar. He sniffed at it. "I knew this would come in handy one day. At least the lighting part."

The harshness of iron painfully grating against stone made Miles jump. He groped into the void for anything. Anything at all. Nothing met his grasp. "That sound! It came from the same corner! Hurry up, for heaven's sake. This is getting creepy!"

"Keep your pants on. I'm doing my best." Wick hunted some more. "Ah-hah!" He found the match and struck it against the nearest hard surface. "And there was light!"

"Wick!" Miles leaped toward his brother. "There *is* a thing! Off beyond the shadows. It's a . . . a body! All hazy and . . . " He began to shiver uncontrollably. Wick shrugged him off a second time as the match burned down to his fingertips and died.

"Blast again! Only one more match on me. Think of something to light, Miles. Otherwise we're doomed."

The thing in the corner moaned piteously, and Miles lunged for Wick a third time. "Even worse! It's alive!"

"Get off me, Miles! How can I do anything when you're acting this way? Where's your scientific curiosity now?"

"This has got nothing to do with science, and you know it! That thing is probably an abomination from the depths . . . a spook, a wraith, a phantasm!"

"All right, so maybe it's Dürer's ghost. Up in arms about what those bund idiots are doing to his reputation. Good grief. Pull yourself together and help me think! What have we got that could give us a reasonable amount of light? Something that might burn slowly?"

Miles sank to the floor, landing limply on his satchel. Inspiration dawned. "My chemistry kit! All the way from the good old United States of America." He kissed the bag's smooth leather. "I knew it would come in handy one day!"

"Hurry up!" Wick snapped. "I've never been in such a fix, in such total darkness. It's much worse than whatever's waiting in that corner over there. Just see what you can find."

Miles fumbled with the clasp and reached inside. "Underwear," he guessed. "Maps . . . *Baedeker* . . . the *Baedeker*!" he shouted. "We'll light a map till I find my tin of all-purpose oil, then pour it over the *Baedeker*. It's thick and dense enough to give us light for ages!"

"That's using your noodle. Here's the last match. Let's do it."

Wick lit the map and watched it flare brightly, while Miles madly rooted for his oil. He got his hands on it just as the flame started dying down. "Too bad about our guide to Germany. If we ever manage to escape, we may never find our way out of the country."

"The book, Miles. Oil the book quickly."

With not a moment to spare, Miles did the deed. As Wick transferred the flame, he dropped back in relief, gaining fresh confidence from the lamp's brightness. "We'll have to twist and oil the dirty underwear next, Wick. Even *Baedeker* won't last forever."

"In due time. Now we must inspect our domain—and our mysterious cellmate."

Another groan escaped into the fetid air. Wick carefully picked up the makeshift lamp, squared his shoulders, and aimed the light toward the figure in the far corner. "Goodness. So that's how they use those manacles. For the arms too. Doesn't look the least bit comfortable."

Their fellow prisoner was hanging from the wall. He was slim and stubble-chinned, ragged and filthy—but definitely flesh and blood. It took a long minute for the truth to register on both brothers.

"My Lord, Miles—"

"It's José Gregorio!"

Nine

Miles flew to his satchel. "Hang on, José! The cavalry has arrived!"

After considerable digging he retrieved a pair of sharp-edged pliers and a file. "First thing we'll have to do, Wick, is get him down from the wall. I don't know about you, but I'd hate to be dangling by my arms that way."

Wick set the lantern on the floor and tentatively approached the prisoner. "José? Are you all right?" He stopped. "Dumb question. Let me rephrase that. Are you all in one piece?"

With great effort the valet managed to nod. Wick edged closer and hesitantly reached up to touch his lolling forehead.

"You don't seem to have a fever. That's a good sign. I suspect you're sore," he rambled on, "and hungry and thirsty as well. Too bad we can't do anything about that. I'm beginning to feel a bit peckish myself."

Miles headed over, whistling between his teeth. "Are you making him comfortable, Wick?"

"Comfortable?" Wick testily responded. "How am I supposed

to make him comfortable? I mean, this is not your everyday situation at the Grand Hotel, Miles."

"Never mind. Here." He handed his brother the file. "You start sawing at those leg things while I work on the handcuffs." Miles stood on tiptoe, then realized the absurdity of his position. "Reverse that order. You're taller than I am."

The two worked in concentrated silence for some length of time. Miles managed to free José's feet just as an ominous flicker caught his attention. He glanced up. "Good grief! I forgot about the light. It's starting to fade!"

Dashing to his bag, he knotted a pair of underwear and doused it with oil, then lit it with the dying Baedeker.

"Golly! That was a close call."

"Quick thinking, Miles."

"Thanks, Wick." He shook his oil bottle. "Not much fuel left. We'd better hurry up with this job."

"Why? José will be more comfortable once we get him down, but then there'll be nothing to do but sit around staring at each other." Wick continued sawing steadily. "For about fifty years or so, depending on the rat population. We can probably do that just as easily in the dark."

"I have no intention of spending any more time in this foul dungeon in the dark, Wick."

"You think old Hans will have a change of heart and save us?"

"Stop dreaming! Any saving, we'll have to do by ourselves."

"How?" Wick finally broke through the first arm manacle. José sighed with relief as the arm dropped to his side.

"By making a bomb, of course," Miles answered. "And not one of my all-smoke-and-no-action bombs either. As soon as we get José down, I'll proceed with it."

Wick glanced at the rapidly burning underwear lamp. "I'll worry about José. You get busy making that bomb."

❖ ❖ ❖

It was early morning when the valet slumped off the wall into Wick's arms. Miles consulted his watch as a matter of record. "Time passes when you're having fun."

"Too much time. Solid iron is harder to file through than meets the eye," Wick muttered.

Miles rewound his timepiece as he watched his brother lay José Gregorio upon the dank floor and gently shove his linen jacket under his head. "We ought to cover him with something, Wick."

"With what? We've burned through every stitch of clothing except our trousers and the shirts on our backs." Wick twitched his shoulder blades. "How's progress coming?"

"Not too bad. Unfortunately, I had to use the satchel for a bomb case. The chemicals have to sit in something. I'm afraid my kit will go up in smoke all at once. No more chemicals." Miles paused from his labors to consider. "I'm only guessing here, Wick. I have no idea how powerful this could be . . . or not be. I've never had the opportunity to do much testing."

Wick sat next to José and absently picked up the valet's hand. He glanced around their cell. "About fifteen-by-fifteen feet square for the main area, I've been figuring, and maybe six-by-ten feet for that little ell at the back, next to where we found José. I assume you'll set the device as close to the door as possible?"

"Yes, but it's all going to go bang at once. With me standing right there doing the detonating."

"But that means—" Wick paused to make the obvious deduction. "I'm afraid that's unacceptable, Miles."

"Why, thank you!" Miles smiled. "I wasn't sure you really cared."

Wick fussed over the valet, averting his eyes. "Well, suppose I do? Things are different now than before we sailed from New York. We never really knew each other before. We didn't share things before. We weren't *friends* before."

Miles bobbed his head. "All true. But there isn't any other way. Unless . . . " He felt in his trousers pockets. "You still have those ropes, Wick? From the first three knots? I've got the fourth one here."

"I think so." Wick pulled his jacket from under the valet's head. "Apologies, José." He handed the lengths of rope to his brother.

"Excellent." Miles grinned. "I knew the knots would be good for something one day. Nice long, slow-burning fuses. This gives me a fighting chance. Now to tie these bits together, attach them to my apparatus, and offer up thanks to Antoine Lavoisier for his gunpowder experiments."

Humming cheerfully, Miles set about his work, leaving Wick to exhale his breath very, very slowly. Shortly, Miles was shoving the satchel up against the door and reaching for the dimly glowing lamp.

"Haul José into the side room, Wick. The ell should give all of us some protection from the main blast."

"Now?"

"Of course now. I'm about to light the fuse! Or would you rather stay imprisoned forever?"

"No, it's just that I thought I had more time to get used to the idea of the big bang."

"The lamp's almost out. It's now or never." Miles lit the end of the rope. "We ought to have at least three minutes—"

"Only three?" Wick began lugging the valet's limp form to the little side chamber.

"*Less!* The rope's burning faster than I expected." Miles scurried over. "Here, I'll help you with his feet."

Hovering protectively over José Gregorio in the ell, the brothers watched their last lantern fizzle into nothingness.

"There goes the light. If your bomb doesn't work, Miles . . . "

"I know. Fifty years of pitch-blackness. Let's hope my science master was right about my potential."

Conversation ground to a halt as they stared at the dim glow of the burning hemp. Halfway through its length, it seemed to splutter and almost die. Wick nervously ran a hand through his hair.

"Have you actually seen any signs of rats, Miles? Noticed any verminlike squeaks? Rat tartare couldn't be that bad, could it?"

"Ssh. Don't talk. Don't even breathe. You can start praying though."

Wick closed his eyes, then snapped them open when he heard a soft hissing sound. "It's catching onto the next knot, Miles! It's going to work!"

The brothers punched each other joyously, while José remained huddled between the two, barely conscious. The rope became shorter and shorter. When the glow stalled just before the satchel on the last Turk's head knot, Miles pushed Wick. "Get down! Cover your head, and José's too! I'll protect his other end."

Wick's arms flew around his head as he shoved his body against the valet's. Miles began to count.

"Ten . . . nine . . . eight. . . "

"What happens when you get down to *one?*"

"Six. . . five. . . all hell breaks loose. Hopefully. Two. . . *one!*"

They cringed in silence. Wick finally stirred. "Nothing's happening! Has something gone wrong?"

Miles pounded him. "Keep your head down, idiot!"

The bomb burst.

✣   ✣   ✣

Wick groaned. He twisted to push a hunk of stone from his legs. "Nice job, genius. You've blown up the entire fortress. And most of it landed on me."

Miles stirred beneath his own pile of rubble. "It worked. It really worked!" He swallowed a lungful of dust and hacked. Next he rubbed his ears. "Louder than I thought too. Do you suppose anyone heard? Anyone above ground? I'd rather not have a welcome committee greeting us. We'd have to go through the entire exercise again."

Wick was rubbing his own ears. "And without your useful bomb kit." He waved through the dark at the invisible miasma of floating grit, then bent to push away more loose debris. "I'll gamble on our being safe for the moment. We're so far underground that the explosion should have gone unnoticed. Also, I don't think any of the Dürerbund people actually live here. They'd have gone home hours ago."

Miles grunted agreement and removed himself from José

Gregorio's legs. "Is he still breathing? You haven't smothered him, have you?"

Wick groped around and managed to locate the valet's head. He lowered his own to listen. "Nope. Actually, he seems to be snoring now. Gently, like a cat."

"Good. Let's see if we can find the way out."

✣ ✣ ✣

It wasn't easy, but they managed to locate the passageway after crawling over piles of rubble while dragging the valet behind them. Wick stood sneezing in the lingering haze of dust outside their cell as he peered into total blackness. He sneezed a final time, swiped a sleeve past his nose, and began sniffing. "This way," he ordered. "The dungeon door was on our right when Erik escorted us here. It's logical to go left. Also, the air seems fresher in this direction."

They hoisted José Gregorio between them, still snoring obliviously.

"He must have been really tired," huffed Miles.

"You'd be too, strung up like he was for a week or so."

"It hasn't been that long, has it?"

As they maneuvered through the passage, they tried to work out how long it had been since the valet had disappeared from Florence. They finally calculated about three or four days. This kept them occupied all the way to the great cavern. It too was pitch-black, but they could sense the air clearing as the space opened.

"Stop," Wick commanded. "Put José down till we figure out how to find the exit."

Miles dropped José's legs with relief. "Thanks. Don't think I could've held him much longer anyhow."

"Don't move. Let me think."

Wick thought.

"If we work our way around the wall to our right, past two giant *Knot* frescoes, there ought to be a sort of corner. Just past the corner should be the corridor leading to the spiral stairs."

"Makes sense. Too bad we're all out of matches. I could fetch one of those incredible candles the bund used last night."

"Forget it. At six feet tall it would just be in our way anyhow. You rested up?"

Miles bent for José's legs. "As ready as I'll ever be."

They carried on.

✣ ✣ ✣

The chamber at the top of the stairs was dimly illuminated by an arrow slit high on the wall of the tower. They deposited José by the skull crusher, and Miles consulted his watch.

"When I began working on the bomb, it was four o'clock. I assumed it was early morning. It must have been afternoon though, because it's after eight now and there's not much light left outside."

Wick sank onto the floor under another instrument of torture. "The darkness probably made us lose all track of time. And it did take awhile to dig out of the dungeon. I suppose we're lucky. Now we only need to wait until it's completely dark, then slip out."

"Slip out to where? We can't very well go back to Frau Hellman's *zimmer*, can we? And we all need some food and water. Especially José!"

As if hearing his name, the valet's mustache quivered. Bloodshot eyes opened. Of his own accord he struggled halfway up on his elbows. "Leave Nuremberg. At once!" His voice was whisper thin but perfectly audible.

Wick leaned closer. "Where to, José?"

"Von Klein's estate." He labored to form the words. "Outside . . . Schwabach." He collapsed again.

Miles and Wick stared at each other. "Schwabach?"

"Where the dickens is Schwabach?"

"I knew we shouldn't have burned those maps!"

✣ ✣ ✣

By nightfall the boys had counted their remaining funds and were checking José Gregorio's pockets for contributions. Wick held up a billfold gleefully.

"No little pearl-handled pistol, brother dear, but the bund left him his money!"

"What did they expect him to do with it in the dungeon?"

"I suspect they didn't care one way or the other. They may be thugs, but apparently not thieves." Wick rifled through the notes. "Francs . . . Lire . . . hah! Some German money at last."

Wick spread out the marks. "I keep getting the exchange rates mixed up, but it looks like enough for a good, long ride into the country and then some." He stuffed the money into his pocket and rose.

"Let's get you and José tucked behind that stairwell, just in case any bund types return to the scene of the crime. You'll have to hold down the fort while I head into town to hire a carriage."

✢ ✢ ✢

Schwabach turned out to be a village some eight miles distance from Nuremberg. By midnight Wick and Miles had found an inn, bedded down the valet, and were begging the innkeeper for food—any kind of food.

Herr Stiegel was not pleased to have been woken from his slumbers, but their money was persuasive. He ladled hot bowls of soup from a pot simmering on the stove. The boys propped José upon pillows and spoon-fed him. Shortly, all three survivors were asleep. They remained sleeping, around the clock and then some.

✢ ✢ ✢

Miles woke at last when he was tossed into a steaming tub.

"What the dickens—"

"Your bath has been prepared, Master Miles!"

Miles thrust his head up from under the water. "José Gregorio! It's really you. You're alive! You're shaved! You're—"

"Clean and saved," finished the valet. "Merely a few remaining aches. Now it's your turn. The innkeeper's wife has kindly laundered and repaired our wardrobes, such as they are. Breakfast is waiting, and so is your brother. It would behoove you to make haste. Time is running out."

Miles snatched a bar of soap. "Running out on what?"

"The fate of Europe. Possibly the fate of the entire world!"

Ten

The boundary of Graf Otto von Klein's estate began a few miles from Herr Stiegel's inn. The three set out cross-country on horses from the inn's stable. José Gregorio reined in his mount when the trail through tight rows of climbing hops suddenly ended. He glanced right and left.

"Nothing but barbed wire fencing. It must enclose the entire property."

Miles pulled up and leaned over his horse's neck. "Why does von Klein need to protect fir trees with barbed wire?"

"We must find an answer to that question." The valet studied the dense forest facing them. "The graf is hiding something in there. Something extraordinary—and dangerous."

Wick prodded his swaybacked nag next to the others. "Let's get off these sorry creatures and find out what it is. On foot."

"Spoken like a man who truly appreciates horseflesh," Miles teased, "who's ready to start his own stables—"

"Enough already, Miles. Every separate jog is torturing my bomb bruises!"

Miles relented. "I guess I'm not in much better shape." He glanced at José Gregorio. "How about you, José?"

The valet shrugged and winced. "Sore shoulder muscles. Not unexpected."

Miles wasn't surprised by the Spartan answer. He was fairly certain the valet—despite his shave and clean clothes—was hurting worse than any of them. After all, hanging from dungeon walls for days must take a toll. Yet if José preferred ignoring the pain, that was his business. Miles moved forward to the dilemma at hand.

"Are you sure the situation is as dire as you claim, José? I know the graf is a little mad. Anyone who could organize that bund ceremony and have us clapped into a dungeon in this day and age has to be a little mad. But I was hoping that once we'd rescued you, well . . . "

"We could just go home," Wick finished.

"We can't go home, because von Klein is more than just a little mad," the valet assured them. "His spies must have been following us from Paris."

"Couldn't you just wire your friends in Scotland Yard and the Sûreté for reinforcements or something?" Wick asked.

The valet shot him a sharp glance. "How did you know about that?"

Wick smiled. "Miles found the secret compartment in your suitcase."

"It seems I haven't given either of you enough credit for your hidden talents—or thanks, either. But we've no time at present for compliments." José Gregorio shook his head. "No, I can't contact the police because von Klein's men control every telegraph station in Bavaria. Perhaps in all of Germany. Our message would never be allowed to pass through the wires."

Miles shoved his glasses up his nose. "So the graf knew all along that you suspected him?"

José spread his hands. "Maybe not that I suspected *him*, but somehow von Klein learned I was a secret agent with the Sûreté investigation. Once that was established, my kidnapping was inevitable. The Dürerbund merely waited for an auspicious moment. Our *pensione* in Florence—with no security like a larger hotel—gave them that moment."

"But why'd they want Wick and me?" Miles asked.

"They didn't. The Dürerbund tried to frighten you off with that little ritual they enjoy—"

"Their knots?" Wick scoffed. "Just piqued my interest."

"And your temper," Miles pointed out.

"*Miles*—"

"When you followed me to Nuremberg, however," José continued, "the die was cast. You'd learned too much."

"Especially after crashing their sacred party in the cavern," Wick concluded.

"True." José Gregorio stared at the forest, but his thoughts were elsewhere. "I overheard enough before my incarceration to believe that Otto von Klein has devised some kind of ultimate weapon. A weapon that will put the world at his feet—with his minions in the Dürerbund trained and ready to keep it there. We have no choice, gentlemen."

Miles pulled something from his pocket. "Well, then, if we have to beard the graf, let's get it over with." He waved a tool at them. "I managed to hang onto the pliers from my satchel. They should get us through that fence."

"Good thinking, Miles!" Wick slid from his horse with relief. "Let's hobble the beasts and get on with it."

✢   ✢   ✢

Miles pushed through the final barrier of trees and stopped cold. "What in the world?"

Wick and José Gregorio peered over his shoulder. A vast, flat, grassy meadow stretched before them—a meadow filled with row upon row of huge, ungainly *things*.

Wick shoved at his lank hair distractedly. "Big balloons? I don't understand."

José shook his head. "I fear I don't either."

Miles readjusted his glasses. "Not just big balloons. Hot-air balloons staked to the ground. . . . Although it's more likely that some type of lighter gas is being used for flotation. Hydrogen maybe? Hydrogen would be more effective than ordinary oxygen, but also more flammable."

Miles took another step forward. "Besides being commissioner of gunpowder, Lavoisier also experimented with methods of cheaply making large amounts of hydrogen for use in balloons way back in 1783, for the French Academy. But the design used here . . . "

He thought hard. "Oval and long, like enormous, fat cigars. Probably less stress moving through the air."

"What are you nattering about, Miles?"

Irresistibly pulled, Miles bolted from the safety of their cover to the closest balloon.

"Wait!" Wick scowled. "That idiot!"

After checking for possible guards, Wick and José followed. Miles was circling the big, open basket attached to the body of the balloon.

"It couldn't be possible," he muttered. "But it must! A motor to the rear. A sort of steering wheel here at the front of the gondola . . . "

Wick shook his brother. "What *is* this?"

"Our mad graf," Miles explained with awe, "our mad graf has built himself an entire fleet of steerable, motorized balloons! Don't you understand? *Airships!* He's invented airships!"

José Gregorio's face turned even paler beneath his dungeon pallor. Showing he hadn't yet regained his strength, he staggered against the wicker gondola for support. "It's worse than I thought. With such a fleet—"

"And bombs," Miles threw in.

"And bombs," José acknowledged, "Graf Otto von Klein could truly enslave the world!"

☩   ☩   ☩

"What's that? The graf's castle?" Wick asked.

They'd worked their way to the far side of the fleet of airships.

An imposing stone edifice loomed beyond.

"It must be," the valet answered. "Possibly twelfth century. Robber Baron Romanesque, from the looks of it." José Gregorio shoved both boys behind the leading ship. "We must take stock. Must think."

"Nothing to think about," Miles responded. "It's evident we've got to destroy the graf's fleet. How, is the question. Fire would be the obvious solution. But to pierce through the outer structure of these balloons, to get to the hydrogen inside. I can't think of a way." He frowned. "Also—"

"Also what, brother?"

Miles sighed. "Also, I'd sure hate to destroy all these beautiful machines before I got a chance to try one."

José stiffened. "Don't even consider such a thing, young man!"

"Why not? How hard could it be to drive one of these? The motor must be started, of course, but after elevation is achieved—"

"No more of this nonsense!" José snapped. "Time is of the essence. First, I must verify today's date. It could be crucial. You rescued me on Sunday, correct?"

Wick considered. "Probably."

"We slept through Monday," Miles contributed. "So today has to be Tuesday."

"Exactly! And it was for Tuesday the graf scheduled his critical meeting at Neuschwanstein. Tuesday evening, in the Singers' Hall."

"Then von Klein can't be here at all!" Miles crowed. "It's miles and miles south to the mountains and Neuschwanstein! There's no way on earth we could get there in time. Unless . . . " He eyed the balloon that sheltered them with renewed enthusiasm. "Unless we took one of these airships for a ride!"

"Out of the question," the valet barked. "It could be death to go up in one of these bizarre contraptions. And if we died, the world would never learn of the graf's schemes."

"But we don't *know* the graf's schemes," Wick pointed out.

"Not exactly. If he went to the trouble of constructing this secret fleet, his plans can't be humanitarian. What we need to know is his schedule—and his target. For that we have to be at the meeting. We also have to discover who his confederates are."

"And we don't mean those idiots squirming around the maze the other night," Miles broke in. "Or the men the bund wasted shadowing Wick and me to leave those knots, either. They don't count."

José strengthened his hold on the wicker gondola. "You're right. They don't count. The entire Dürerbund must be only a curtain, a red herring. Certainly, the troops formed by it could be useful . . . not to mention the total, unquestioned loyalty von Klein appears to have achieved through his Dürer cult. Yet—"

"Oops." Miles ducked. "Don't look now, but I think our graf is still at home. At least, a carriage just started out from the entrance of that twelfth-century fortress of his. And it's heading this way."

It soon became evident that more than a carriage was on its way. The open vehicle was followed by a score of men, marching in quickstep. Wick and Miles exchanged glances.

"I think von Klein plans to attend his meeting tonight in style, Wick."

"I think you're right, Miles. And those men must be coming to set his airship aloft."

"What do we do next?"

"Hide!" José ordered. Then, as an afterthought, "But try to watch how it's done, Miles. Please?" His pallor became a deathly hue. "Duty might require that we make an attempt at flying after all."

Miles grinned. "My pleasure entirely."

✢ ✢ ✢

The four matching horses—as coal black as the lacquered carriage they pulled—pranced to a halt beside the front-rank airship. Two soldiers smartly goose-stepped to the carriage door, which was adorned with Dürer's hare like a heraldic device. They saluted, and the graf stepped to earth. His leonine head and hawklike profile were vivid in the midday sun as he reviewed his domain with regal pride. A figure who almost eclipsed von Klein alighted next from the vehicle.

Concealed behind the third balloon to the rear, Miles choked. "It's our art dealer. It's Pierre Polisson!"

"I don't believe it," Wick yelped. "Has he been involved all along? Even back at the *biergarten?*" He quickly clamped his jaws shut. José Gregorio might distinctly disapprove of their frequenting such a place.

The valet ignored Wick's slip. "I suspected the man for a villain all along. His painting provenances were doubtful, his manner oily and obsequious—"

"Ssh. They're looking this way!" Miles bent lower. "You're nearest the corner, Wick. Can you manage some discreet spying? I need to be able to follow their preparations for flight."

"I'll try." Wick carefully edged around the gondola. "I think it's safe for the moment. The graf is showing off his baby, walking the entire circumference. . . . Now he's giving Polisson a hand into the gondola carriage—"

"Sorry. Gotta see." Miles yanked his brother out of the way. "The helpers are forming a circle around the ship. Each is hanging on to a piece of the rigging. . . . The graf just climbed inside the gondola too. Along with another man—he must be the captain; he's got sort of a nautical cap on his head—yes, he's moved to the front, by the wheel. . . . A fourth man is clambering aboard. He's going for the motor in the rear. I've got to get closer to watch how he starts it!"

"Wait, Miles!"

Wick shot out a hand to catch his brother. Too late. Shaking his head, he inched forward to watch Miles's slight figure dash the distance between their airship and the second one—the one closest to the graf's. He breathed more easily when Miles made shelter.

Meanwhile, von Klein's men—seized with the excitement—burst lustily into a marching tune, which further incited their ardor. Clutching the rigging, they stamped out the beat with their glossy knee-high boots. They were making such a row that it took Wick a moment to realize yet another sound had been added to the din. He tore his eyes from the men to study von Klein's gondola.

"The motor, José." Still watching, Wick tugged sharply at the valet's arm. "They're trying to start the motor!" Getting no response, he glanced back. The valet was clutching his arm in agony. Puzzled, Wick stared as José slumped to the ground. "What's the matter?"

José Gregorio rolled his head, shielding the arm with his limp body. "I fear those manacles injured me more than I realized. My shoulder . . . feels torn from its socket. . . . Too much effort, too soon . . . "

"But you've been fine all morning! You got us going again!" A terrible thought struck Wick. "It wasn't that tug of mine just now, was it?"

"You had no way of knowing. Nor did I. . . . Apologies . . . " A spasm crossed the valet's face and his eyes fluttered shut.

"You can't do this to us, José!" Wick cried.

"Alas," the words came in short gasps, "you and Miles. . . must take over. . . again. I have complete . . . confidence . . . in your abilities."

"José!" Wick shook the limp body before he remembered the results of that last little tug. He backed off in confusion. "This isn't the way it's supposed to happen. It's *your* job to save the world, not ours!"

There was no response.

✛ ✛ ✛

Oblivious to the drama behind him, Miles concentrated on the uniformed figure hovering over the motor of von Klein's airship. Squint as he might, he was still too far away to distinguish critical mechanical details. Without thinking, he clambered into the gondola sheltering him. In seconds he was crouching by the motor, parallel to the graf's. Hanging from the inside wall of the woven basket was a pair of binoculars.

"Excellent," he muttered as he lifted them and made the necessary adjustments. Von Klein's machine popped into close focus. "A fairly straightforward engine. Shouldn't be too hard to start. A little pull here, a little push there . . ." Unconsciously, Miles's free hand was shadowing the movements of the graf's engineer. "Ease up on this clutch lever . . . "

Otto von Klein's airship engine roared to life.

✧ ✧ ✧

A wild cheer from the riggers distracted Wick from tending to José Gregorio.

"The engine's started!"

He watched in fascination as the graf's men pulled rigging stakes from the ground—one by one, almost ritually. As each stake was released, its rigger grabbed for his freed length of rope with one hand and smartly saluted von Klein with the other. When the circle of ropes was loosed, the graf shouted a single order.

"*Schiff hoch!*"

The airship began to rise.

The gondola hovered ten feet, then twenty feet above the riggers. Von Klein leaned over the side. He clipped out a string of words, but only one drifted back to Wick.

"—*Vaterland*—"

The reply hit Wick's ears like a tidal wave:

"*Vaterland!!*"

At last the airship took control of its destiny. It tore rigging from tightly clenched fists and rose higher—graceful and free. Wick's jaw hung ajar. He was hypnotized by the sheer beauty of the thing as it negotiated a complete turn in the sky. That was when Wick saw the hare emblazoned within a maze on the side of the balloon. He raised his fist and shook it skyward.

"You've caught poor Albrecht's rabbit, von Klein, but you won't catch the world in the same trap!"

"Wick! Wick! Pipe down! Are you trying to get us captured again?"

Wick spun around. "Miles!" He dropped his fist in embarrassment. "I guess I got carried away there—"

"It *was* fairly epic, but we've no time to lose. Not if we want to keep the graf and Polisson in view. Following them is our only hope for getting to Neuschwanstein. At their present rate of speed through clear skies and over mostly flat fields, I'd calculate—" Miles stopped to work out the problem. "—I'd calculate that gives us half an hour. After that their airship will be completely out of sight."

"Half an hour to get airborne and follow? But what about von Klein's helpers? We can't do a thing with them hanging about!"

Miles nudged his brother in the direction of the castle. "They're already trotting off for home. Not wasting any time about it either. I suspect they mean to make hay while the sun shines and their leader is gone." He turned back. "Where's José?"

Wick motioned behind him.

Miles took in the sprawled figure. "I won't even ask what happened. There's not a second to spare. First things first. We haul José into airship number two. Then we figure out how to dismantle the rest of von Klein's fleet."

"How are we supposed to do all that in thirty minutes? *And* take off?"

Miles consulted his pocket watch. "As Uncle Eustace would say, *twenty-nine* minutes."

Eleven

With little ceremony the boys hoisted José Gregorio into the gondola of the second airship. Miles rubbed his hands. "Phase one of our mission completed." He readjusted his spectacles. "Now for phase two . . . "

A frenzied braying stopped him in midsentence. He spun toward the noise. "What next?"

Wick grinned at the comedy unfolding at the edge of the forest. "Looks like a very angry farmer chasing a runaway donkey."

"*Zum Teufel!*" The man's fury and frustration echoed clearly across the vast field. "*Zum Teufel!*"

"Amazing the way you can always remember the more interesting bits of vocabulary. He's calling the poor beast a devil. How does he expect to catch him, lugging that pitchfork and scythe?"

Wick and Miles watched the man halt in confusion. His head twisted uncertainly between the escaping donkey and the unaccountable objects moored before him.

"He couldn't be one of the graf's people, Miles. He's acting as if he's never seen these airships before."

"And it's got him totally bewildered," Miles agreed. "I'll bet his donkey snuck in through our hole in the fence, and he chased after it, and—"

"*Schwarzer Teufel!*" The farmer began howling anew. Now the object of his wrath was the nearest balloon. He went at it with his pitchfork.

"Superstitious lot, these peasants." Wick smiled. "He probably figures the graf's airships are responsible for his donkey's bolting. Isn't happy about it either."

"Wick!" Miles pounded at his brother. "The solution!"

"Would you stop hitting me like that all the time?" Wick rubbed his shoulder in irritation. "What solution?"

"Don't be so dense! Our farmer came with the right tools. All we have to do is borrow them, pierce each balloon, then set fire to the farthest one. The hydrogen will ignite. In fact, it'll blow sky-high, better than any of my bombs. All the others will catch too!"

Wick whistled. "And the graf's fleet will be destroyed—except for our pursuit ship . . . hopefully. What're we waiting for?" He took off after the peasant.

As the farmer viciously attacked the bloated skin of the farthest "Black Devil" with his pitchfork, Miles tore at shreds of the balloon's outer shell to peek inside. Luckily, the farmer was too possessed to notice him.

"Poor luck. The gas is kept in a separate envelope, with a space between it and the outer shell. We'll have to burst that inner envelope."

Wick picked up the farmer's fallen scythe. "I love it. My one chance to send modern science directly back to the Dark Ages!"

"I'm not sure I approve of your sentiment, Wick."

"You're the scientific genius, Miles, not me." He began slashing. "There's one blow for physics . . . and one for chemistry . . . and another for biology . . . "

"You're getting your disciplines mixed up, Wick."

"Out of my way!" Wick slashed until he heard a hissing

sound. He stood back, puffing. "That ought to do it. Got a match, brother dear?"

"What about the other airships?"

"If this stuff is as lethal as you claim, they'll destruct all by themselves."

Miles fished in his pockets until he remembered. "Hey, you're the one with the matches!"

Wick dropped the scythe. A wry smile crossed his face. "And I used them up in the dungeon. Great. Now what?"

"*Hee-haw!*"

"Hey!"

Wick stumbled as the donkey returned to butt him aside and head for his master. The farmer froze, pitchfork in midair, when he noticed the boys for the first time. The pitchfork fell from his hands.

Wick caught his balance and raised his arms in peace. "No hard feelings over your beast. Match. Have you a *match*? To light a fire . . . Oh, what the dickens is the word for *fire*? If I ever live through this, I swear I'll spend the rest of my days becoming a linguist! No more of this dumb American nonsense."

Ignoring his brother, Miles smiled his friendliest smile at the sweating, gaping farmer and calmly made the gestures of stuffing and lighting a pipe. The man nodded in sudden comprehension.

"*Feuer. Ja.*"

He removed a long wooden match from a pouch at his waist and handed it to Miles. Miles mimed broad, move-away motions with his arms till the farmer caught the message and took off for the woods, his donkey in tow.

"Start sprinting, Wick. Fast as you've ever run. You've got to save José, in case my calculations are off. This is going to be worse than my little bomb in the dungeon. Much worse."

"Now?"

"I said *now*!!"

Miles struck the match on his shoe, waited for its flame to steady, then flung it into the balloon shell and raced for his life. A sudden stillness held the air, as if the entire sky were imploding. A muffled crack broke the stillness, and intense heat billowed out to follow him.

The invisible force seized Miles and flung him forward to land on both feet, still running. He caught up with Wick, and they dashed for the balloon where they'd left José. It was their only escape route.

A series of explosions pursued them across the field, like titanic bursting kernels of popcorn—each eruption coming nearer. Would they make it safely? Would they manage to lift off in time, before the final airship joined the conflagration of the others?

"The stakes, Miles." Wick huffed by the final airship. "Help me pull 'em up, then hop into the gondola. Better yet"—he was already tugging madly—"jump in now and start that motor. I'll follow soon as I can."

Miles didn't argue. He leaped aboard, tripped over José's inert body, and stumbled to the engine.

"Push here. Shove there. Ease up on the clutch. Please work. *Please* start."

Nothing happened. A quick glance to the field behind proved there was but one unexploded airship between themselves and oblivion. He attacked the motor with renewed vigor. "Push here, shove there, ease up on the clutch . . . " The motor chugged to life.

"*Yes!* Wick! Wick? Where are you?"

The balloon began to rise.

"*Wick!!*"

"Help! . . . Man overboard!"

Miles frantically raced around the perimeter of the swaying gondola until he found a piece of rope still taut. He peered down.

"Wick! What are you doing hanging onto the rigging?"

"I *said* start the motor, Miles. I assumed you'd wait for me before taking off!"

"Sorry. I haven't figured out how to control the ascent yet." Miles hauled in the line. "Hang on. Don't let go."

"I know I've spent fifteen years trying to prove otherwise, but if you think I'm stupid enough to let go of a lifeline fifty feet above ground. . . . "

Miles looked down at his dangling brother. "We're rising faster than expected. A hundred feet, Wick. And at the present rate of acceleration—"

"For heaven's sake, just pull! My fingers are slipping!"

Miles pulled until he was certain there wasn't another pull in him. Luckily, a final heave brought Wick's head into view. "I'm letting go of the rigging. Grab for my hand."

"Are you sure you can catch it?"

A tremendous explosion snapped their attention downward. The last remaining balloon had just been incinerated. Its flames spouted up in an inferno worthy of an erupting volcano.

"Good grief! Those flames are going for my feet!" Wick leaped in midair and caught the rim of the gondola. In a moment he'd toppled head over heels to land squarely on José. "Accelerate! For goodness sake, now's the time to accelerate!"

Miles raced back to the motor. "The steering wheel, Wick! I need direction!"

With another mighty effort, Wick crawled the length of the open cabin to the wheel and used it to haul himself up. He spun it. "Is this the right direction? Are we clear?"

Miles tore himself away from the engine to study the ground below. "Yes. I think we're clear of the fires." He squinted ahead. "Can you see the graf's airship, Wick?"

"Are you serious? It's a wonder I can see anything. It's a wonder I'm not blind! I think my eyelashes are singed. Along with everything else."

Miles remembered the binoculars. He rammed them to his eyes, forgetting his glasses. Mercifully, his lenses didn't break. He scanned the field first.

"There's that farmer, hanging onto his donkey for dear life at the edge of the forest. I'm really glad he escaped." He swung the binoculars. "Gosh, but we made a proper mess of the graf's fleet. There'll be nothing left but charred and twisted struts."

He moved the binoculars again. "And it looks as if von Klein's men have finally noticed the commotion. They're pouring out of his castle like ants." He twisted the focus. "Oh no! Not that!"

Wick was struggling with the steering wheel. "What is it, Miles?"

"Von Klein's men are pointing guns at us!"

"Terrific. A few bullets through this flimsy balloon shell will have us erupting like the ships on the field below."

"Too true." Miles continued reporting. "Now they're beginning to actually shoot!"

"Can't we shake that engine into more speed?"

"It's out of my hands, Wick. It only seems to go at one speed."

"Then we'd both better start praying."

Wick and Miles ducked as gunshots cracked around them, while the airship slowly, ponderously made its way across the sky. It seemed they were under siege forever. In reality it was only seconds before the sounds of the shots became fainter.

"Phew." Wick swiped at the sweat running down his face despite the coolness of the higher altitude. "Out of range at last. That was a close call." He reached for the wheel again. "About following the graf? Remember? I think we're veering south, toward the mountains. But it would be nice to know for sure."

Miles shook his head. "How about checking the compass tucked beneath the wheel?"

"Compass? Oh."

"I'll just make sure." Miles raised the binoculars once more and pointed them in what seemed a southerly direction. "I think . . . maybe . . . *yes!* We're charting the right course. Look up ahead, Wick. That speck. It's too big for a bird. What else could be floating through the sky?"

"It must be von Klein's airship."

Miles lowered the binoculars. "Phases two and three complete. Destruction and pursuit. I think we've done it, Wick. On to Neuschwanstein!"

Twelve

As the airship neared the mountains, the earth below turned from flat fields to rolling hills. Miles abandoned his motor to stand beside the wheel in the gondola's bow.

"How are we going to recognize this castle when we see it, Wick?"

"I'm hoping it will be fairly obvious. Presumably it's the only castle around."

"There's always the graf's airship too," Miles speculated. "He's got to set it down somewhere close. That should be an unmistakable landmark."

Wick adjusted the steering wheel a few inches. "Speaking of landing, have you given it any thought yourself?"

His brother nodded. "I've been working out calculations for the last hour or two. I estimate we're cruising at almost twenty miles an hour, and we've been airborne more than five hours. At that rate . . ."

"What are you hesitating about, Miles? Have you found a solution or not?"

"In point of fact, Wick, it's not crystal clear how to lower this thing." He shrugged. "I mean, we could just turn off the engine and see what happens, but at twenty miles an hour, that'll still give us a certain amount of drift."

"And there's no one waiting to catch all that rigging hanging from our sides."

"You thought of that too."

"So what do we do? Drift till we bump into the nearest mountain?"

Miles sighed and gazed over the side. "I just don't know. We've figured out that the wheel is connected to the rudder, but that only moves us left or right. There's probably some sort of vent at the top of the bag to let out gas for descending, but with all this upper rigging floating around—besides the mooring lines—I'm afraid to mess with the wrong thing and have us descend too soon." He smiled. "The truth is, I wouldn't mind going on forever in this airship. The view is spectacular. Can't you imagine flying clear across the Atlantic Ocean and home in it?"

"Right. To land in our garden. That would give Mother a thrill."

"I don't know about Mother, but Father would certainly be excited." Miles's eyes sparkled with the thought. "He'd love something like this for his expeditions. Can't you see him cruising above rain forests and wild rivers, stopping when he spots an interesting specimen?"

Wick shook his head. "For a budding scientist you've a god-awful romantic streak. At the moment we need to be more practical. We're up here"—he peered down to the earth—"and the ground is several hundred feet that way. *Hard* ground, I might add. Also . . . " Wick glanced ahead. "Also, I can't make out the graf's airship anymore."

Miles reached for the binoculars hanging from his neck. "You're right. It must have disappeared through that notch in the mountains dead ahead."

"Seriously *growing* mountains, Miles. A whole range of them. Probably the beginning of the Alps. And the wind is picking up too. Here, try this wheel for a minute. It's getting harder to hold steady. What if we can't steer our ship through that gap? What if it chooses to follow the air currents straight into the side of the closest peak?"

Miles took over the steering from his brother. In a moment he was hunching into the wheel with his entire weight. "This is tougher than it looks!"

Wick nudged him aside and regained control. "Right. I'm finding muscles in my arms I never knew I had. It's way easier steering Father's yacht in Long Island Sound . . . although this really is a lot like a boat. . . . " Wick paused. "Wait a minute. Maybe it's more like a boat than we thought."

"What do you mean?"

"Have you had a chance to check the piles of ropes scattered about the gondola? Could there be an anchor attached to one of them?"

Miles blinked. "You mean to fling overboard and catch at something solid below?"

"Exactly," Wick agreed. "At least it might give us a chance to settle this ship in one spot. After all, we don't have any riggers to help us." A spluttering sound distracted him. "Was that the engine? Maybe you'd better get back to it."

Miles whipped around. "No, the engine's steady. But José Gregorio isn't. Looks like he's staggered to life at last—and is retching over the side."

"Good. At least the back-to-life part. We'll need his help when we arrive."

✦ ✦ ✦

The sun began its descent as the boys maneuvered the airship between the mountains. Having gotten better at adjusting the ship to the air currents, Wick and Miles were enjoying the panorama spread out before them. José Gregorio was not. The valet was shivering in a tight fetal ball midway between the two sides of the swaying gondola. Apparently, heights did not appeal to him.

"Here you go, José." Miles bent to tap his shoulder. "I found a water canteen. Have a drink."

"How did we get up here?" The valet groaned. "And what happened to the rest of the fleet? On second thought, I don't want to know." He waved away the water. "Just disappear. Allow me the courtesy of dying in peace."

Miles sipped thoughtfully from the canteen. "Wick told me about your shoulder socket. Is it any better now?"

José very cautiously twitched it. "Yes . . . actually, yes."

"Maybe when we slung you into the gondola, it reconnected itself. How about the air sickness? Has that improved?"

Another groan was the valet's only response.

Miles continued to study him. "I don't understand, José. I mean, you're the soul of competence in civilized situations, but . . . well, you do seem to fall apart when things turn a little nasty."

José moaned in agreement.

"You can't be blamed for that unexpected arm business, of course, and we'll have to keep an eye on it, but what I'm really getting at is—"

"Stop being so diplomatic, Miles," Wick called from his steering post. "Spit it out."

"All right, then." Miles spit it out. "How in the world were you ever recruited by Europe's top police agencies?"

José Gregorio made a noble effort at straightening his body, but the gondola's swaying motion soon had him curled more tightly than ever. "The worst decision of my life." The words escaped from beneath the arms covering his head. "They needed an art scholar and linguist. A man of refined tastes. I was certainly all of those. . . . Living a happy, *quiet* life. Disturbing no one."

"And?"

"They trapped me while I was on sabbatical at Oxford." José

uncovered his head to lean on an elbow. "In a moment of weakness, a moment of boredom with my scholarly existence, I allowed myself to be recruited."

"But how'd you learn all that valeting stuff?" Miles broke in.

"Yes, how?" Wick was curious too. "You've got that subservient yet patronizing attitude down pat."

"I *was* educated in England," José protested. "And my original family home in the Argentine was not without position," he continued. "Or suitable staff. My grandfather was a great general of our revolution . . . Perhaps that had been gnawing at me. The desire to prove that I too could be a man of action."

"Well, I guess I can understand part of that," Miles commented.

"Like Miles and me," Wick added, "trying to prove ourselves to the family."

"A not unsimilar situation, now that you mention it," José agreed. Concentrating on the words seemed to take his mind off his discomfort. He sat up. "At any rate, I was placed for a month under the tutelage of a superior valet of the English aristocracy."

"And then?" Miles prodded him further.

"By then . . . everything had been set in motion. Scotland Yard's agents had already zeroed in on potential American millionaires likely to be making the Grand Tour for art purchases. They suspected all along that the key to the Dürerbund might be art. It was inspired by one of the greatest masters in history, after all." He grimaced. "Your uncle just happened to be the right decoy at the right time—and he had the financial resources to swell the movement's coffers with his purchases."

"Hah!" Miles exclaimed. "So Polisson was always the middleman."

Wick turned from the wheel. "How did the police get rid of Uncle Eustace's old valet?"

"Paid him off. Forged my papers. Ferried me across the ocean and put me in place in New York. . . . And everything was fine until Florence. Until I walked into the *pensione*'s hallway from your uncle's room to find myself gagged, tied, rolled in a rug—a very *dusty* rug—and spirited off to Germany." José shuddered and pulled his knees up to his chin. "Enough. I want to be alone."

Miles returned to his engine. He was beginning to worry about a possible fuel shortage when Wick cried out.

"Dead ahead! Castle in sight!"

Miles scampered to the bow. "Where? Oh! That's got to be Neuschwanstein. It's an absolutely perfect castle!"

Neither brother noticed the valet stagger up behind them. "A sham castle is what it is. Built by mad King Ludwig a mere thirty years ago."

"José?" Wick turned from the sight. "Are you feeling yourself again?"

Even in the dying light the green hues of the valet's face were impressive.

"I've had better days."

"So it really is *Neuschwanstein*? We've found it?"

"You could hardly miss it, Miles, sitting as it is astride its own little mountaintop. Only someone as insane as Ludwig could choose *Schloss Neuschwanstein* as a symbolic meeting place."

"Golly, José," Miles protested. "I sort of like it. It's what I always thought a European castle *should* look like, before I saw the real things. All those wonderful towers and turrets—"

"*Bah*. A toy. A fairy-tale castle."

"You guys better stop arguing about the architecture and start thinking about landing," Wick interrupted. "Down below there, in the valley. It's the graf's airship."

"All neatly battened down," Miles observed, "with not a soul around it. Or anywhere else, from the looks of things. It's all amazingly, frighteningly quiet. Even the wind has died." He scanned the area. "The valley's not very big either. Most of it's taken up by that lake just below the castle. There's not a lot of space left for us to land."

The sun dropped rapidly behind a nearby crag. Its final rays reflected off the bright stones of the tallest towers of Neuschwanstein.

"It'll be too dark to land in another few minutes!" yelped Wick. "What about that anchor you found, Miles? Think fast!"

Miles studied the castle they were nearing at an alarming rate. "Only one thing to do," he finally said.

"What?" Wick hugged the steering wheel, trying to decide whether to overfly the soaring castle, or skirt to one side of it.

"It's obvious. We moor our airship to *Neuschwanstein* itself."

José Gregorio's complexion shifted to a deeper shade of green.

✢ ✢ ✢

"Anchor ready, José?"

They were cruising at an altitude not more than fifty feet above Neuschwanstein. Wick aimed the airship at the pointed cone of its highest tower. "Careful with your bum arm, but remember we've only got one chance. I don't know how to reverse this ship!"

José Gregorio took a deep breath, tightened his hold on the anchor rope, and risked a look overboard. He blanched, gagged, then caught himself. "Ready!"

"Cut the engine, Miles!"

Miles pulled a lever. "Engine full stop!"

Wick clutched the wheel as the distance narrowed between themselves and the tower. "Steady, steady . . . anchor away!"

The valet hoisted it by its steel shank and swung it over the gondola's side. The three watched as it plunged through the deepening twilight to jolt to a stop at the end of its line. There it swung—only inches from the weather vane surmounting the tower. In maddening rhythm the anchor swayed back and forth, back and forth, its flukes neatly evading the goal.

"Catch!" Wick yelled.

"*Please*," Miles whimpered.

The arc began again. Back and forth . . . back and forth . . .

until a slight grating noise drifted up to them. The airship plowed forward, jerked . . . hesitated . . . and stopped.

"Done!" Miles whooped. "We're moored to *Neuschwanstein*. Now all we have to do is climb down one of these ropes—"

José Gregorio swayed with the motion of the gondola. Wick and Miles just managed to catch him in their arms as he slumped once more.

"I don't think he takes after his grandfather the general, Wick."

"Nope. It seems as if we'll have to plan the next stage of the mission ourselves. Again."

✢ ✢ ✢

Miles slid down the rigging first. Thankfully, there was no wind, but still the rope wobbled crazily with his weight. He shimmied past the weather vane, purposely not looking at the little copper flag whose slim rod anchored their airship. He knew it would also be the castle's lightning rod, so its fragile appearance had to be deceiving. Still . . .

A yard below, he kicked out and touched the slates of the tower's cone-shaped roof with his shoes. Another yard, and he spied his destination through the falling night. It was a narrow, crenelated balcony jutting out just below the eaves of the roof. fingers slippery with nervous perspiration, he continued to shift one hand under the other, pause for a beat, then repeat the process.

"Monkeys do it all the time," he whispered. "Monkeys in Father's jungles. Who ever heard of a monkey losing his grasp and falling from his vine?"

Slide . . . grip . . . slide . . . grip.

"I've got the same opposable thumbs. I can do it too."

He kicked out once more. Squinting through the gloom, he saw the edge of the balcony, with a window in the tower wall just beyond. Excellent. That meant it wouldn't be necessary to scale the other three hundred feet of the tower to the courtyard and a door. "Only another yard . . . get some momentum going for the leap—"

He landed neatly inside the balcony.

"Good job, Miles!" floated down from above.

"Thanks, Wick!" Miles rubbed a damp hand on his trousers. "Gosh. It *was* a good job," he murmured to himself.

"Now tie your end of the rope to something. With sturdy knots. Dürerbund quality."

"Aye, aye, captain!"

Miles got busy. In a few minutes he had a strong lifeline fastened to a block of stone projecting from the low parapet wall. He glanced up. "Have you attached the safety ropes to José?"

"Yes," Wick answered. "Trussed up fore and aft. Better yet, he's awake again."

"Ship him down!"

Wick hoisted the valet over the side and aimed his hands at the taut rigging. "It's up to you now, José. I'll be taking the pressure from your arms, but you'll have to guide yourself. If you fall I can catch you with these ropes around your chest, but you'll have to work your way back to the rigging again. Understand?"

José Gregorio nodded numbly and reached for the main rope. Contact made, he tightly shut his eyes and began working his way down.

"He's doing it blind, Miles! You'll have to grab his legs when they come within reach!"

"Understood."

Miles positioned himself for the capture. José was making things even harder for himself, inching down like a snail. "Come on, José," Miles cheered. "I have faith in you. You can do it!"

There was no answer, but the valet's creeping pace picked up. Miles heaved a sigh of relief when he could finally lean over the balcony and touch the man's feet. "Open your eyes now . . . Good. Look this way. . . . A nice, sturdy balcony is waiting for you. In a solid building, on a solid mountain. Another few inches, José, and you'll never have to tackle heights again."

The valet's legs wriggled into Miles's grasp. In a brief moment he was over the top, hugging Miles fiercely.

"Safe and sound," Miles assured him. "But let go of the rigging, please. And me too. We've still got to get Wick down."

Miles pried José free. Then it was Wick's turn. He slithered down the rope with aplomb and landed on the balcony with a grin. "That was fantastic! When do we get to do it again?"

"Never!"

José Gregorio had plastered himself to the rounded wall of the tower, as far as possible from the balcony edge and its yawning drop to the castle courtyard below. His breath came in ragged gasps. "Please, gentlemen . . . if you'd be so kind. . . . Lead me to shelter!"

Thirteen

"Stand clear, men!" Wick ordered.

The tower window had proved impossible to open.

"Ready, aim—" He kicked.

Almost before the glittering shards exploded onto the balcony, José Gregorio was slipping between the jagged edges. Miles followed.

Wick dallied for a moment on the balcony, taking in the shadowy outlines of the castle below, the moon beginning its rise over a distant mountain, and finally, their airship still hovering above. The wonderful invention that had brought them so far floated ghostlike in the night.

"I can't believe it's real," he murmured.

Miles stuck his head through the broken window. "Can't believe what?"

"Our airship. It looks like a dream up there. No one will ever believe it existed. That we did what we did in it."

Miles gazed up admiringly before a thought occurred to him. "According to the gauge, there wasn't enough fuel to take us much farther, Wick. The beauty got us exactly where we needed to be. Yet . . . do we really want the graf to see it floating above the castle? To get his hands on it again? To use it for his evil schemes?"

"Not on your life!" Wick paused. "But I can't bear destroying this one like the others in von Klein's field. Not after having piloted it halfway across Germany. It behaved so nicely for us, seemed almost alive." He paused again. "She doesn't deserve that."

Miles edged back onto the balcony. "*She?* You're making her feminine, like a boat?" He considered. "Well, why not? And she does deserve a reward. Let's set her free, Wick. To go where she wants to go."

José reached through the window to grab at Miles. "That abomination might be our only means of leaving *Neuschwanstein!*"

Miles turned toward the valet. "You'd be willing to climb back *up* the rigging, José? With your shoulder ailing? To take another ride in the airship?"

"No! I mean, I don't think I could manage it, even face it. . . . "

"There's your answer." Miles joined Wick at the balcony's edge. "I made the knots. Why don't you loose them?"

An almost full moon now illuminated the balcony and the lone strand of rigging. Wick worked quickly. "There." The rope danced free in his hands. He gave a few sharp yanks.

Miles craned his neck toward the top of the tower and the weather vane. "Give the rope another tug, Wick."

Wick tugged and Miles smiled. "That's done it. She's free. Beginning to sail off farther south."

"Fantastic! To have that kind of liberty, to be totally unfettered—with everything before you. No masters at all!" Wick smiled too.

"Are you both satisfied?" The grumble came from within the

safety of the tower. "May we get on with saving the world now?"

Wick grinned at Miles. "José Gregorio's definitely on *terra firma* and taking command again!"

✢ ✢ ✢

José led the way down the tower's spiral staircase. "I've been here before to study the paintings," he explained. "I was beginning a book on German Romanticism. But the pictures are all derivative, the lot of them. King Ludwig was obsessed with German mythology and Richard Wagner's operas, in equal doses. Wait till you see the murals in the Singers' Hall. The legend of Parsifal all over the place—"

"José?" Wick interrupted.

The valet rounded another spiral. "Yes?"

"We didn't really come here to continue our art educations."

José stopped. "It's all connected. Don't you understand that yet? You can't begin to fathom the directions of contemporary history until you see what it's working from. The Dürerbund could not exist if a few modern Germans weren't as obsessed as Ludwig was over building a great, mythic past for the country. And if such a past never existed, then it must be invented." He struck the stone wall of the tower well. "Fairy tales! They're trying to build greatness from *fairy tales*! Just like this castle!"

Miles nudged his brother. They'd paused by another window in the tower, and pale moonlight lit their bodies. "Do you suppose José's nanny told him even scarier fairy tales than ours did?" he whispered. "He doesn't seem to have a warm spot in his heart for them."

"Could be." Wick snickered as an image crossed his mind: an image of a tiny, primly mustachioed José coiled at his nanny's feet. "We'd best distract him." He raised his voice slightly. "When do we get to this Singers' Hall, José?"

The valet moved on. "I've never actually been in this particular tower before, but I know it opens onto the fourth floor of the palace. That's where the hall is. Von Klein's meeting place. We'd better make as little noise as possible from here on in case he's posted guards."

Another half-dozen revolutions brought them close to an open archway through which soft light glowed. José held them back. "This should lead to the Anteroom of the Singers' Hall. I'll see if it's safe to proceed."

He merged into the shadows, then sprang to the archway, barely edging his head around its corner before retreating.

"Soldiers—several score of von Klein's personal guards standing at attention inside the Anteroom!"

"Now what?" Wick murmured.

"We'll have to slip through the archway and look for the stairway to the third floor. It's just to the right, nearly out of sight of the guards. From there we'll go through Ludwig's private quarters and return up the servants' staircase. It opens onto a long gallery overlooking the hall. We should be able to observe the meeting from the gallery." He paused. "Remember, we've come only to *observe*, not disrupt."

"Sure," Wick commented dryly. "Just like in the Dürerbund's cavern in Nuremberg. That's how we were caught the last time."

Miles shook his head vehemently. "I refuse to set foot in another dungeon!"

"Ludwig didn't include a dungeon in his castle plans," José assured him. "I've no interest in seeing another myself. Come. Time is passing as we argue."

Wick and Miles followed the valet to the archway.

"Down!" he ordered.

They crawled on hands and knees past the entrance to the Anteroom. Wick glimpsed rings of candles burning from candelabra, illuminating the vibrant colors of wall murals. Miles kept his eyes down, counting the black-clad legs of the soldiers. There were more than enough to scare him into a spurt of speed.

Safely within the next stairwell, José guided them down to the third floor. He paused at its entrance and took stock.

"Von Klein's had all the main rooms illuminated. Probably for atmosphere. Good. Also good that he's neglected to post any guards down here—at least no obvious ones. We'd best make for Ludwig's chambers while we have the opportunity."

Cutting across the open space, the valet ducked into a doorway to one side. The boys followed and met pitch-blackness once more.

"I guess the graf didn't expect to give any tours of the private quarters tonight, José." Wick groped for the nearest wall so he wouldn't trip over anything. "But I'm a guy who likes a little light."

"Me too," Miles agreed. "After that dungeon there's something about total blindness that doesn't appeal to me."

José gave in. "Fetch a candle, Wick. From one of the wall sconces in the hallway. Quickly!"

Wick obeyed, returning with a foot-long taper gripped firmly in hand. "Lead on, José!"

They'd discovered another kind of labyrinth. One opulent room wound into the next, treasures shimmering to either side of their flickering light.

"The adjutant's room. The servants' room. The dining room." José announced each. "Ludwig's study." He paused for a moment. "Take note, gentlemen. Wagner's minstrel-knight Tannhauser— all over the walls."

Wick held the candle under the nearest mural. He whistled softly. "Who's his gorgeous friend?"

"Venus unveiled. Tannhauser's temptation and downfall." José stepped closer. "I detect a trace of Rubens here . . . "

Miles pushed on through a draped doorway. "Hey, guys!" he called back. "Forget the nude. There's something much more interesting in the next room!"

Wick moved the candle away. "How can you tell in the dark?"

"I can *feel* it. Something really strange!"

"Ludwig's grotto," the valet explained. "With a secret door to the servants' staircase. It's what we've been seeking." He urged them on.

"Wow!" Wick exclaimed. He held the candle high in the new chamber. "How'd he get a cave up here on the third floor of the castle?"

"With stalactites and everything!" Miles added in awe.

"Merely oakum and plaster of Paris." José sniffed. "Another outrageous outpouring of the romantic spirit in vogue at the time."

"But I really like this cave! It's a nice, cozy size. With its high ceiling and things dripping mysteriously all over the place—"

"No time for misplaced admiration, Miles. Search the rock for the hidden door."

The three groped their way across the rough outcroppings of the wall between stalagmites and stalactites. Miles edged up to a small, flowing waterfall—and yelped with pain.

"Ow! I've got my finger stuck in a crevice and it won't come out!"

José Gregorio rushed over. Instead of releasing Miles, he inserted his own fingers above Miles's imprisoned one. "The hidden doorway. You've found it!" As he exerted pressure, an entire section of the wall—waterfall and all—slowly, steadily shifted toward them.

"*Voila!*" José Gregorio smiled. "Neatly hidden from prying eyes. The servants' staircase!"

❖ ❖ ❖

"What do you call it when it feels as if you've been somewhere before?" Wick was flat on his stomach, peering between two of the ornate plaster columns bordering the gallery above the Singer's Hall.

"*Déjà vu,*" José whispered.

"I've got the same feeling, and I don't like it one little bit," Miles complained.

"Hush. Both of you. We're listening to the last movement of Bach. Von Klein's musical entertainment for his guests should end momentarily. He couldn't resist going for the grand gesture in this space. But soon he'll need to get down to business."

True to the valet's words, the chamber orchestra at the far end of the ceremonial hall completed its last flourishes and acknowledged the applause from the seated audience. As the musicians drifted offstage, Von Klein himself rose from a bench and held up both hands before his assembly. When he spoke, it was, surprisingly, in English.

"I am sure all of you—my honored guests—have enjoyed listening to this music from Germany's great cultural past. But we've gathered in this magnificent hall not only to remember the past. More importantly, we have come to speak of the future.

"From the windows of this *schloss* you were privileged to observe my arrival in a most auspicious vehicle, the *von Klein Airship*! In a matter of hours it brought me across Germany. Only consider how and *where* the remainder of my fleet will be able to transport armed men—under cover of darkness—in a single night!"

The graf's audience stirred in their seats. It was a smaller group than Wick or Miles had expected after their experience with the Dürerbund in Nuremberg. Perhaps twenty men were gathered within the grand space, perched uncomfortably on delicate, gilded chairs set before the stage. None of the men were costumed—but neither was the graf.

Instead, Otto von Klein stood before his audience in a simple suit, graced merely with be-ribboned decorations hanging from his neck. If anything, the simplicity of his attire accentuated his hawklike nose and roughly sculpted face to better advantage.

"The ability to navigate the air is nothing less than a turning point in history, gentlemen. It is the most important invention of modern times." He paused to gloat. "And I control it! In the future the history of mankind will be divided into periods before and after this conquest of the heavens; before and after the Confederated Empire of the Air we have met here to finalize! The future of Germany, the future of your own countries—allied with our newly established confederation—lies in the *air*!"

Von Klein bowed, waited for the storm of approval to subside, then began mingling with his guests. As the men rose, José Gregorio—lying between Wick and Miles—grew agitated.

"What's the matter?" Wick murmured.

"Toward the front of the group. It's the head of Britain's opposition party! And the French undersecretary for foreign affairs!" He shook his head in disbelief. "Behind them is a leading Italian diplomat, and one of the Austro-Hungarian Empire's chief spokesmen!"

"That's not all," Miles added. "There's our buddy Pierre Polisson, right in the thick of things. What's he doing?"

Pierre—Van Dyke beard freshly combed, satin cape furled—strode to one side of the hall and clapped his hands authoritatively. Twice. Liveried servants answered his call, entering the room with trays of fluted glasses, opened bottles, and hors d'oeuvres.

"Champagne," the valet breathed. "Polisson is acting as the graf's majordomo."

The crowd seemed to relax with the refreshments. They were comfortably chatting now. Von Klein raised his own glass and faced them again. "Before we reconvene for our last round of negotiations, gentlemen, may I propose a toast?" The graf waited for nods of assent.

"To victory!" he trumpeted.

"Nuts," Miles groaned. "We really did miss most of the important part. All we're picking up is leftover stuff."

"Wait," José cautioned him.

The graf downed his wine, plucked another glass from a waiting attendant, and toasted again.

"To September first! The lowlands! Then to follow the footsteps of Caesar himself—across the Channel . . . next, the world!"

"September first!" All glasses were raised.

"That should do it," Wick stated. "A date, a target, *and* the identity of the conspirators. Enough information for you, José?"

He turned to the valet. "Because I think we ought to get out of here before we're caught—"

"—or before the graf finds out about his destroyed fleet, and *then* we're caught," Miles finished.

José Gregorio began easing himself toward the gallery's exit. "Hold on—" Wick was still spying from his vantage point. "It might be too late already."

José hastened back in time to watch a very large uniformed man race into the midst of the proceedings below, dragging a terrified peasant behind him. "That soldier looks quite familiar . . . "

"Of course he does," Wick agreed with resignation. "It's Erik von Klein, the usual bearer of ill tidings."

✣ ✣ ✣

The three of them made it back to the servants' rear staircase as chaos broke loose. Shouts, marching feet, even a few gunshots pierced the sterile air of the castle.

"We've been discovered!" Miles gasped.

"Not yet," Wick clarified. "It was lucky José understood the German back there. That peasant only reported sighting our airship moored to *Neuschwanstein*. Von Klein suspects spies on the loose, but he'll have to telegraph his family manse back north for details. Meanwhile, what's our next move, José?"

"Head for the grotto. It's probably the safest place at the moment. We'll hide there and wait for things to calm down."

"Let's do it fast," Miles breathed. "I hear footsteps right behind us!"

✣ ✣ ✣

They tumbled down the stairs and through the secret doorway. As it shut behind them, Miles pushed against it, somehow hoping his slight body would be enough to hold back the hordes. He was so intent in waiting for pounding fists and shouts of outrage that he didn't even notice the waterfall splashing his shoulder. Only after the sounds of pursuit moved past their secret door and farther down the staircase did he jerk his body away. "It's cold!"

"And dark again." Wick sighed.

"'Weep, for the light is dead,'" mourned José.

"What's that supposed to mean?" Miles asked.

"Nothing . . . and everything. Schiller, a great German poet, once wrote those words. If we do not manage to escape, if we are caught—they could prove true."

Wick snorted. "Aren't you overdramatizing the situation just a tad, José? I mean, von Klein may have his grand Confederation of Evil all lined up, but Miles and I did cramp his style by blowing up his entire airship fleet."

"And now he'll never be able to begin his attack on September first," Miles smirked.

"True. But a man like the graf will see that as only a small setback. In a few days he'll have his minions beginning the construction of another fleet. There is tremendous energy involved in madness. . . . And if we are captured before we relay our information, who will be left to hold back the darkness?"

Neither Wick nor Miles had an answer to that question.

Fourteen

"*Neuschwanstein* stands nearly on the southern border of Germany."

José Gregorio was blindly pacing between the walls of the grotto. Hours of darkness had turned the cozy space claustrophobic. "Somehow we must make our way over the mountains to Austria, thence through Switzerland to France—and finally Paris, to make my report."

Wick sprawled against a rough wall, legs splayed out before him. "So we have a little hike through the Alps." He yawned. "What's the big deal? Once we're out of Germany, we're home free anyhow."

José snorted. "Obviously you've never hiked through the Alps. In my salad days I did a little of it—on the lower slopes—for sport. I assure you, Wick, even in high summer these mountains are not to be toyed with."

Miles drank from the waterfall, then splashed his face. "You guys are forgetting that we have to get out of this castle first. It's amazing we haven't been discovered yet, the way the graf's troops have been clumping up and down the back stairs for hours."

"And searching through Ludwig's private quarters. It's a miracle they didn't make it this far," Wick added.

"True," the valet agreed. "But we cannot presume our luck will last forever. It will be dawn soon. . . . Surely most of the night has passed. . . . If we don't attempt our escape before morning, I fear we'll be stranded here another day."

"Getting hungrier and hungrier," Wick complained.

"And weaker and weaker," Miles pointed out. "I can't remember when we ate last. If those mountains are as tough as José claims, I vote we make a stab at 'em sooner rather than later. Now, while I can still sort of move."

Wick tried getting up, then slumped back again. "What's the point? Surely by this time von Klein will have guards posted at every strategic pass out of this valley."

"Just as he'll have his men," the valet added, "or the men of his allies at post offices and telegraph stations throughout every surrounding country."

"Come on, José," Miles protested. "He can't have *that* many in his organization!"

"I couldn't vouch for followers of the non-Germans in the alliance, but already the Dürerbund has more than half a million members."

"Half a *million?*" Wick asked.

"All looking for us," Miles moaned, as he searched for the groove of the door next to the waterfall. "It's been quiet out there for a while. Let's get moving before the graf hauls the entire bund to *Neuschwanstein* to begin scouring the mountains."

Miles barely cracked the secret door before slamming it again. "Another bunch coming down the stairs!"

"*Ssh.*" Wick's lethargy fled. "On our rear flank! We're being invaded through Ludwig's study!"

"Hide behind the stalagmites!" hissed the valet.

"There's not enough space for all of us!" Miles wailed.

Wick and José ducked behind the row of artistically arranged cones they'd seen earlier by candlelight.

In desperation Miles scrambled past the waterfall and up the side of the wall itself, blindly feeling for footholds in the cracks and crannies. When the light of a torch flooded the cavern, he found himself sheltered by a series of descending stalactites. He crouched within an indentation in the wall, trying to quiet his breath. But nothing could quiet the heartbeats pounding wildly in his ears. Surely they could be heard throughout the entire castle.

"I tell you, they are here somewhere!"

The voice was hard to forget. Miles forced himself to look down. The sudden light was almost worse than the hours of darkness. It was Erik von Klein! And—

"Calm yourself, Erik. There are more important things to search for than a few brats. Politics change, my friend." The voice was a soothing purr. "But art—art is forever!"

"So easy for you to say, Polisson. You are not my father's son."

Polisson shivered. "I am not. And perhaps it is time for you to break the familial bonds too. Already you've watched your father squander the funds I've channeled to the organization—"

"After taking your commission."

The dealer shrugged. "A businessman must live. More importantly, you've watched your father squander most of your inheritance. *Your* inheritance, Erik. *Your* money. On what? Those quixotic airships of his."

Polisson paused directly below Miles. If the stalactites had been real they would be oozing moisture onto his lush mane of hair.

"And what happens? A little accident and *poof*—" Polisson snapped his fingers. "They have disappeared. Up in flames and smoke, Erik. *Your* inheritance."

The graf's giant of a son stood facing Pierre Polisson. He gripped the torch angrily.

"*What* accident? It was those Americans! And their spying valet—the man you yourself reported to my father! They are to blame for everything. Blowing up the dungeon. Destroying the ships! If that peasant with his donkey had not been caught, had not been convinced to tell my father's men what he witnessed—"

"Perhaps you're right, Erik," Polisson soothed.

"And the other peasant here," von Klein raged on. "With his tales of a balloon tied to the highest tower of Neuschwanstein. I can hardly believe it! I want my revenge, Polisson. I shall have it!"

Polisson stepped toward the giant. "Don't be so thick, my friend. Revenge may taste good on the palate, but it leaves the stomach empty. At least your kind of revenge."

"There is another kind?"

Polisson took the giant's elbow gently. "Of course, my friend. Of course. Being very, very rich is a most excellent revenge. And never has there been an easier way."

He moved Erik toward the exit of the cavern. "Let me remind you of my American millionaires, Erik. About what they will pay for European art. The Dürerbund may have established the gallery in Paris, but the contacts are *mine*. After this confederation nonsense has passed, excess funds can be channeled into *my* pockets—and those of a future partner. There is still much art to sell, Erik. The kind of art your father has cluttering up his castle. Art such as Ludwig is reputed to have hidden in this absurd *schloss* of his."

Polisson waved his arms airily as they neared the far door. "Not this silliness on the walls, Erik, my friend. Oh no, indeed. *True* art. Dürers—"

"Dürers?" Erik halted at the name he could understand.

"And not mere woodcut knots, either. Engravings. . . drawings. . . perhaps even a missing portrait or two. Somewhere in this *schloss*, Erik."

Pierre stretched his arm companionably around the giant's shoulders. "If I were to be given a little assistance here at Neuschwanstein—and with the odds and ends at your father's estate, of course—I believe a most prosperous partnership could be formed." The two wandered out, taking the light with them.

After a suitable period of silence, Wick whistled low and clear. "So that's why Pierre's been hanging around Nuremberg and the graf! And why José got kidnapped to start with."

"All is explained at last," agreed José Gregorio.

"Leave it to good old Polisson to figure out how to take advantage of the Dürerbund's craziness," Miles added. Then he remembered his precarious position. "How in the world do I get down from here? I feel like a bat!"

"Grab one of those stalactites and swing down, Miles," Wick said. "Fake or not, this whole place is sturdier than it seems."

"Well, if you think so . . . " Miles grabbed with each hand for the points directly in front of him. Catching a firm grip, he let out a little whoop and swung free. The stalactites swung with him. "Whoah. Hey, guys!"

"Just let go, Miles," Wick called through the blackness.

"No. There's something strange happening. I think another piece of the wall just came away with me."

"We mustn't leave any evidence that we were here, Miles," warned the valet.

Miles was still swinging. "You don't believe me!" He finally dropped with a soft thud. "*Oof.* Well, I'll get a little more light on the subject."

"Miles, no!"

But Miles had already felt his way to the study entrance. Barely pausing to check for danger, he grabbed a candle from Ludwig's desk and hopped on the thronelike chair. Lighting the candle from the chandelier von Klein's men had kindled sometime during the night, he scampered back to the grotto.

"There! Why we didn't think of this sooner—"

"We were trying to *hide*, dimwit!"

"Boys. Enough." José snatched the candle from Miles and thrust it toward the stalactites.

"There *is* something back there." He edged closer. "A carefully hidden compartment devised to open as the stalactites are pulled outward. It's certainly large enough to contain . . . "

Miles was already clawing his way back up the wall—with Wick close behind.

"Can you hold that candle closer, José?" Wick called as he peeked around his brother. "There're a bunch of papers in sort of a safe here."

"Let me look at one, Wick."

Nudging Miles aside, Wick glanced at the top sheet. "At last! One of Dürer's knots!"

"Is it like the frescoes in the cavern? Let me see!" Miles begged.

"Wait a minute . . . " Wick thumbed through the pile. "Something even more interesting!" He shifted a paper out and passed it down.

José Gregorio stared at it in silence.

"What've we got, José?" Miles asked.

The valet tore his eyes away with difficulty.

"*Eureka!*" he whispered. "*Eureka!* We've found Ludwig's cache! Knowing the knots are here is wonderful, but they are only prints. This . . . this is an exquisite drawing by Dürer himself." With a shaking hand, he held the candle closer to the image.

"His very signature. To hold something of such significance . . . *Women's Bathhouse*. This picture has been lost for several hundred years!"

Both boys leaped down to crowd around their find.

"Gosh!"

"I suspected our Albrecht did more than cute little rabbits," Wick allowed. "Not bad nudes."

"Not mere *nudes*," the valet chastised. "Nakedness in Renaissance art meant so much more. Such beauty was never only skin deep. It signified purity and innocence."

Wick made an "if you say so" shrug. "So how do we get it out of here, José? How do we get all of that art out of here?"

The valet lowered the drawing with a sigh of regret. "We don't. We return this piece. Very carefully. And we close the secret compartment. The art has been safe here for ten long years since Ludwig's death. It should remain so for another little while."

"But, but—" Miles protested.

"But nothing. This collection is not ours to take. We are neither thieves nor pirates. Perhaps later, after properly cataloging the pieces. Studying their provenances. Determining if a legitimate owner still exists." He sighed once more. "Perhaps then our discovery might allow us certain rights. For the moment, by trying to escape with these works, we might only destroy them forever." José Gregorio shook his head. "We cannot carry this art across the Alps. We will be fortunate to carry ourselves."

"Couldn't we at least look at the rest of what's up there? Find out if there's a complete set of knots?"

The valet studied Wick. "I thought art bored you."

"Not *this* kind of art. Not anything by our Albrecht!"

José smiled. "All right then, but quickly!"

"It's my turn." Miles scaled the wall to the trove. He'd barely touched the pile when the sound of approaching footsteps returned. "Oh no! Not Pierre again. He can't have these! He won't!"

"Over my dead body!" Wick snatched *Women's Bathhouse* from the valet's hands and shoved it back toward his brother. "Close it all up! Fast!"

Miles worked in a frenzy, pulling the stalactites toward him as José snuffed the candle. Wick and José scurried to their earlier hiding places, while Miles crouched back into his rough cubbyhole.

". . . Then we have an arrangement, my dear Erik?"

The torch floated by Miles's feet.

"First I must make a show of aiding my father in this spy business, Polisson."

"Of course, of course. But do try to capture the brats alive, my friend. They are worth significant sums in ransom. And there are millions more down the road in art sales."

"For Dürer, I will tear this *schloss* apart with my bare hands!"

"Certainly. After the capture. But all should be accomplished with discretion, dear boy. Discretion."

The two disappeared again.

Miles dropped from his perch. "As much as I hate to leave Albrecht's art, somehow I think my skin comes first."

Wick dusted off his trousers. "I'm not convinced about Erik. I don't believe he truly knows the meaning of *discretion*. Especially if he gets his hands on us again."

José Gregorio took shape in the gloom. "Homicidal maniacs do not change their stripes for mere money. Let us depart with haste, gentlemen. Our escape we will leave to our wits and heaven."

✢ ✢ ✢

The servants' staircase ended in the kitchen. It was large and empty, but there were signs of recent activity.

Wick inspected the space. "Where do you suppose the cooking staff is?"

"Probably hunting for us, like everyone else. Say!" Miles picked up a discarded apron. "We could disguise ourselves as kitchen help!"

"Excellent thought." José began wrapping a huge apron around his slim body.

Wick, meanwhile, was busy shoving scraps of food into his mouth. "*Mmph.*" He swallowed. "They were working up to a regular feast. Would you look at that side of beef on the spit. And suckling pigs too!"

Miles studied them longingly. Their juices were flowing over crisply crackling skin. As his hollow stomach growled, he snatched a carving knife and flew toward the open fireplace. The valet stopped him.

"There isn't time! Stuff your pockets with that bread and cheese on the table—"

A noise made them all freeze.

"Someone's coming!" Miles whispered.

They ducked in three directions, under three separate tables.

"—I tell you, Herr Graf, it won't do!"

Wick peeked from his hiding place to note that the speaker was the Englishman José had pointed out from the gallery.

"The spies must be caught at once! Should my name be released, I'll be ruined!"

"You are being anticipatory, Malcolm. My men have the situation well in hand. There is no way they can escape."

"But you don't even know their identity!"

"On the contrary. It would seem our *spies* consist of two simple American children under the tutelage of this San Martin. And he must be crippled by earlier tortures to which my men subjected him."

"I begin to question this organization of yours, von Klein. If two lads and a cripple can create this degree of havoc—"

"Bah! A fluke! They understand nothing of what has occurred here."

"According to that telegram you received, they apparently understood enough to destroy your entire airship fleet—"

"Causing only a slight delay in our agenda. It is being rebuilt as we speak. . . ."

The voices faded. Miles emerged from his shelter. "I don't care for the graf's attitude. *Simple American children!*"

"*Lads!*" Wick came into view. Without wasting time he spread one of the aprons on the floor and began loading it with food. "Europeans have no understanding of what Americans can accomplish when they set their minds to a goal. We crossed the seas to conquer the New World, didn't we? We crossed three thousand miles of wilderness to conquer the West, didn't we? Just let them try to keep us from crossing a few Alps!"

Wick tied the apron strings to make a parcel, then rolled up his sleeves and knotted a soiled napkin around his neck.

"That knife in your hand, Miles. Hang onto it. It could come in handy. And grab a basket and fill it with wine bottles while you're at it. We've some thirsty work ahead! José—" Wick turned to the valet. "What're you staring at? And why in the world are you taking time to uncork that wine?"

A small *pop* was followed by a thin, wry smile. "Only trying to match your efficiency, Wick." He slipped the corkscrew into a pocket. "Bribery is a highly underrated European pastime."

Wick didn't even try to understand. He snatched at an abandoned chef's cap and set it rakishly upon the valet's head. "Well, if you're finished, sling one of those pigs from the fire over your shoulder. It's the perfect cover for a *cripple*. The troops are getting hungry, and someone has to feed them, don't they?" He darted his eyes around the kitchen one last time. They stopped at a bowl of flour.

"Ah. Final *bona fides*." He dipped a fist into the bowl and liberally anointed all of them with flour down to their shoes. "We're the new catering team. At least until we get across the castle courtyard and through the gate."

Miles grinned as he knotted a napkin around his own neck. "So much for our wits. The rest is up to heaven. Let's get this show on the road!"

✛　✛　✛

Despite his display of confidence, Wick almost quailed when they reached the outside door. Dawn had not yet broken, but the courtyard was ablaze—courtesy of dozens of von Klein's torch-bearing soldiers.

"It's your turn, José," Wick whispered. "You know the language. Concoct a good story if they stop us."

The valet, hunched under the suckling pig, nodded. With an effort he straightened his slight body and set out as if he owned the place. Wick and Miles followed, making a show of their own burdens. They made it halfway across the open space before a voice cried out.

"*Halt!*"

José spun toward the soldier and let loose a barrage of German. Even without understanding a word, Wick and Miles caught the valet's scathing tone. The soldier backed off and waved them forward.

Crossing the rest of the courtyard under the eyes of the remaining troops took an eternity, but eventually they were at the gates, facing another set of guards. José stopped to readjust his burden. Freeing a hand, he plucked a wine bottle from Miles's basket. He presented it formally to the sergeant at arms with a little speech. Wick caught something about "the graf's compliments to his faithful and vigilant soldiers" before the sergeant pulled at the loosened cork with his teeth, spat, and tipped the bottle to his lips. Escape from Neuschwanstein was achieved.

Fifteen

Halfway down the mountain, the liberated group heard more guards climbing up the narrow dirt road. They darted into the woods and froze, moving only when the men marched safely past their hideaway. José dropped his burden, unwound yards of cloth, and cast apron and chef's cap aside.

"I refuse to carry this pig another foot. The heat has burned through my clothing and seared my very flesh. As for my shoulder—"

"Oh say, I'm really sorry about that," Wick apologized. "It seemed a reasonable solution, and you carried it with such aplomb that even I forgot—"

"It had to be done. But we cannot count on the stupidity of too many more of von Klein's guards. Continuing this disguise any further might press the point."

Miles already had his knife out and was carving the meat. "No problem. None at all. We'll have breakfast right here. We'll leave what we can't swallow or pack."

"Then take off through the woods." Wick smiled. "That

largish hunk will start me off perfectly, Miles. Now I know what people mean when they say they could eat a horse!"

✛ ✛ ✛

José Gregorio navigated by the moon falling in the west and the sun rising in the east. It became easy to head south. By mid-morning they'd put one small mountain between themselves and Neuschwanstein. When the valet called a halt next to a rushing stream, they quenched their thirsts. Then Miles pulled off a shoe to massage his toes.

"I wish you'd had the foresight to insist we all dress in boots that last morning in Florence, José. These silly things weren't made for mountain climbing."

"Neither is this ridiculous white summer suit." Wick brushed distastefully at the remains of his jacket.

"As for the suit, Wick . . . " the valet spared a tiny smile, crinkling his pencil-thin mustache. "I believe it to be faultless. It is now so concealed by stains that you blend in with the summer forest."

"Gee, thanks." Wick smoothed a ripped lapel. "Moldy dungeon green, grotto black, and a lovely burnt sienna from the airship explosions. Wouldn't the fellows at school be impressed."

"Possibly not. But a few of the Old Masters might. You're carrying a veritable palette of pigments on your person."

Miles wrinkled his nose, and his glasses slid. "That was *awful*, José!"

He shoved his spectacles back and returned to the more important things on his mind. "At least we've figured out how to bypass the graf's troops. They make so much noise tromping through the woods that only a halfwit would run into them."

"For the moment," the valet agreed. "Soon, however, von Klein will send professional mountaineers after us." He rose. "Then our mettle truly will be tested. Come. Look above and beyond, gentlemen. There you see *real* mountains."

Miles pulled on his shoe and squinted into the distance. "Good grief." He polished his lenses with a clean square of the apron he'd tucked into his basket. "Snow? In July?"

"Snow all year long, Miles. Only on the other side of that snow will we find Austria and safety."

⁘ ⁘ ⁘

Hours later, the three were still hiking due south, but the sun had long since begun to settle into the west. It had taken all day to break through the tree line of the first range of snow-capped peaks.

Wick hobbled to a stop. "It's going to be dark soon, José. We can't keep climbing all night, can we?"

"Perhaps *someone* could, but not me." The valet collapsed next to a clump of alpine flowers. "We'll have to sleep here. We must find a crevice, some sort of shelter from the night wind."

"It has gotten even chillier, hasn't it?" Wick rubbed his hands together briskly, then checked the sky. "And I don't like the look of those clouds massing on the horizon either."

"Rain?" Miles wondered.

"At this altitude, snow," José corrected him.

"Maybe we should go back down into the trees," Wick suggested.

"Did you hear those odd sounds not half an hour back?" The valet didn't wait for the boys to answer. "Dogs. They've set dogs on our trail—and beaters behind them, undoubtedly. We're no longer being pursued by amateurs."

"Don't dogs need a scent to follow?" Wick asked.

The valet had begun to study the tiny white flowers with intense concentration. He finally looked up. "My apron and chef's hat."

Miles cleared his throat and changed the subject. "What exactly are beaters?"

José sighed. "A beater is a person engaged to rouse game. A number of them are set out in a line, half a dozen yards apart from one another. They beat every foot of ground between them with great sticks. Grass, bushes. Nothing escapes them. When the game flees in a frenzy, the hunters—strolling just behind—start shooting."

"Oh." Miles blanched.

"That's hardly sporting," Wick complained. "And I don't like being thought of as a stupid partridge or grouse!"

José stood. "*Au contraire*, Wick. Hopefully we're the fox. He leaves a scent but can still outwit his pursuer."

He began pacing while he contemplated their grim options yet again. "I'm afraid we'll have to climb higher and pray for the bad weather to come soon. Rain—or snow—will slow our pursuers. Search for a true cave. There should be some around here. In Austria the mountains are tunneled with salt caverns."

Precious minutes spent poking into every outcropping proved fruitless. Wick gave up as harsh barks sounded loud and clear through the thin air. "Those bloody dogs. They're closing in faster than we can outthink them!"

The valet held up his hand for silence and listened. "Only a few minutes grace. We must abandon this side of the mountain. Quickly! Perhaps the far side will be more hospitable!"

Wick and Miles followed José, limping in their tattered shoes, their parcels of food and drink from Neuschwanstein becoming more burdensome with each step. Damp, clammy mists began to settle around them, making it harder to find their way across the rubble near the peak. Suddenly, José Gregorio disappeared from view. Wick stumbled into Miles.

"Where's he gotten to?"

"Not sure." Miles was puffing. "You notice how hard it's becoming to breathe up here, Wick? It has to be the altitude. The oxygen isn't as dense. There've been studies made of altitude sickness, you know. It comes on after extreme physical exertion—"

Wick grabbed his brother's arm. "Save the lecture. We have

to find José, have to stick together. After what we've survived, it would be ridiculous to lose each other now."

Miles didn't complain, just trudged forward. Around another outcropping of rock, he stopped. "The mist's lifted, Wick. Is that José up ahead?"

Wick hadn't even noticed the valet. His own eyes were focused on something just beyond. Something large. Something *huge*, bouncing placidly on the very brink of the mountain's edge. His hand tightened on Miles's arm. "Tell me I'm seeing things, Miles. No. Tell me I'm *not* seeing things!"

Miles rocked on his blistered feet. "If we're not dreaming, it's the most beautiful thing I've ever set eyes on. *She's* the most beautiful thing in the world!"

Their airship stood before them, patiently waiting. José had already broken into a run. Wick and Miles followed at a gallop.

"The wind's picking up!" Wick yelled. "Grab the rigging before she goes over the edge!"

All three leaped wildly for the fluttering ropes. Each barely grabbed one as the airship began to tug loose from its precarious resting place.

"Into the gondola, Miles!" Wick ordered. "I've had practice hanging in midair!"

Miles tumbled into the wicker car, wine basket first, then turned to help the valet. "Eyes open this time, José!"

With a commendable effort of will, José Gregorio managed the maneuver. The gondola shifted dangerously beneath them, half on, half off the mountain.

"Come on, Wick! Your turn!"

Wick flung his bundle of provisions toward his brother as the gondola bottom scraped against the peak's rough shale. He caught a rope with both hands and focused on his haven. Then the baying began. High-pitched. Resolute. Maddening.

"Good grief!" Wick swiveled to look. "It's a hound from hell!"

It was—and there were others closing in behind: a whole pack of huge, broad-shouldered, slavering beasts. The airship rose to float over the abyss below as the closest animal, unwilling to lose its quarry, launched into space with a mighty leap. Its open jaws snapped—

"He's got his teeth into my trousers!"

Miles hung over the rim and began reeling in his brother. "Kick him off! But don't lose your grip! You can do it. You're much closer to the gondola than last time, Wick!"

Wick shook his leg furiously. "Last time there were no fangs attached. Hurry up!"

Behind Miles, José Gregorio rushed to the rescue. "Two will be better."

Wick jerked his leg a final time. The hound loosened its grip and fell back among its comrades. Amid the angry snarls and mournful howls that rose to the heavens, Wick finally made safety.

"Thanks, fellows." He grinned up at them from where he lay sprawled on the floor of the basket. "A situation like this makes you really feel wanted."

"Of course you're wanted," Miles shot back. "You're wanted at the wheel to steer *Gretchen*."

"*Gretchen?*" Wick struggled up. "I had in mind a more flowing name. *Esmeralda*, for example."

"She's German, isn't she? She ought to have a German name."

Wick laughed. "Fair enough. See if you can stoke up the young lady's engines. There's probably another peak hiding behind that mist dead ahead. It would be awfully nice if we missed it."

José Gregorio remained leaning over the airship's side, queasily staring at the fate they'd so narrowly escaped.

✤ ✤ ✤

The fluffy pillows of clouds closing in from all directions seemed to comfort José. Instead of curling into his usual airborne ball, he began to make himself useful. While Miles tinkered with the engine, he neatly arranged the provisions they'd managed to save. Next he began tidying up the rest of the gondola. Under a large, untouched pile of ropes, José made his discovery.

"Miles?"

"What is it?" He was bent over the motor, trying to cajole it into life.

"I've found a large metal container." He twisted off the cap. "It doesn't smell like water—"

"José!" Miles rushed over to stick his nose into the spout. "Fuel! You've found us some fuel!" He hugged the can to his chest and staggered back to the engine. Within a few minutes, Wick and José heard a sweet, steady puttering. Miles fiddled some more, and the airship began to rise higher.

"I've finally discovered how to adjust the tail planes!" he crowed. "It gives me some control over the altitude!"

"Just in time," Wick yelled back. "Go as high as you can! I can *feel* another mountain coming at us!"

Gretchen rose to the situation like a true lady. Shortly, the airship was breaking through the cloud cover, flying just above the peaks below. Wick began to breathe naturally again. "What direction shall I set the compass for, José?"

The valet glanced up from the meal he was fixing. "West. Make for true west, then see if you can tie the wheel in position and join us for a few minutes. I have a little picnic prepared."

✛ ✛ ✛

Perhaps it was the food after such a long day. Then again, it was probably the wine José Gregorio shared with the little group to make up for the lack of water. Two bottles of it. Miles closed his eyes first.

"I believe I've worked out why *Gretchen* was waiting for us," he murmured. "She's lighter than air. As her altitude increased, the air density decreased. . . . Meanwhile, the temperature dropped. . . . Anyhow, her engine sounds fine. . . . I'll just rest for a moment. . . ."

Wick succumbed next.

The valet made a circumference of the ship, listening to the engine, peering at the compass in the bow to make certain they were still heading west. Finally, he covered the boys with their aprons from Neuschwanstein. Realizing they were poor protection against the frigid air, he carefully bundled them within coils of hemp rigging. Neither boy stirred.

After studying his charges for another long minute, the valet curled up between the two and gave in to sleep himself.

Sixteen

Miles was the first to awake. He struggled from his cocoon of ropes to stretch mightily. Glancing over the side, he noted that the sun was not only up but nearly overhead. He fumbled in his pocket for his watch and held it to one ear. Miraculously, it hadn't stopped. He wound it and wandered to Gretchen's pounding engine, then began calculating time and mileage. When his companions woke at last, he'd reckoned a fair estimate of the distance they'd traveled.

"I think we've been flying about sixteen hours, Wick." He nodded to the valet just behind. "At almost twenty miles an hour, that makes about three-hundred and twenty miles we've done."

José was astonished. "But if that is the case—" He inched to the side of the craft and cautiously peeked at the clear view below. His face didn't turn nearly as green as during their earlier flight. "It's unbelievable! We've slept through Austria and Switzerland. We must be over France!"

"France!" Miles shouted.

"We're home free!" Wick slapped his brother on the back.

"Now you're pounding *me!*" But Miles didn't complain, just danced around the gondola caught in his brother's bear hug. The celebration ended when Miles detected a subtle difference in the engine's vibrations. He raced to the rear of the gondola.

"*Gretchen!* How can you do this to me! We're nowhere near Paris yet!"

Wick ran to the wheel at the bow. "Has she gone fickle on us?" he called back.

"No," Miles answered. He studied a wildly fluctuating gauge. "Just hungry again. And this time we've nothing to feed her. How far to solid land, Wick?"

Wick studied France undulating in the sunlight beneath them. "We've been flying higher than ever before. Maybe a quarter of a mile."

"Prepare for a fast descent!"

✢ ✢ ✢

But *Gretchen* remained a lady. She decorously lowered herself through the sky until she was floating about fifty feet above land. Then she paused—as if choosing the perfect spot—and settled primly to the ground. A few gentle bounces, and *Gretchen* was still.

"That's my girl!" Wick gave her sides a parting caress as he clambered from the gondola.

"She deserves more than a pat, Wick." Miles threw a kiss to the airship as he hit solid earth.

"Gentlemen . . . if you please . . . "

José still clung dizzily to the basket. Wick poked his brother. "Shall we rescue him a final time?"

"Why not?" Miles laughed.

✢ ✢ ✢

Rescued and reacclimated, José Gregorio studied the terrain.

"So," Wick asked. "Where do you think we are?"

The valet shrugged. "Somewhere in the heart of France. In the middle of some farmer's pasture." He pointed toward a curious cow slowly ambling in their direction, then inspected the distant fields. "Wine country, maybe. There seem to be vineyards over there."

Miles was squinting through the midday sun in the opposite direction. "And there's water that way. At least a little ribbon of it. A river?"

José Gregorio went to retrieve their remaining provisions. "I suggest we find out."

✣ ✣ ✣

It was a canal. They sat by its banks and lunched on the last of their bread and cheese.

"The Canal Lateral, perhaps?" José guessed. "Or another. It hardly matters. Eventually, all the canals connect to rivers that will take us to Paris." He stretched. "We need only beg a lift from the first boat we see."

"It's either that or walk," Wick said. "Seems as if you'll get that barge ride you wanted after all, Miles."

"Me? When did I say that?"

"About a million years ago back in Paris. Don't you remember? The morning we first visited the Louvre."

Miles ruffled his hair thoughtfully. "Maybe I did. We'll have to find a lock, then. A barge won't stop for us in the middle of nowhere."

Wick rose. He smoothed the dog-shredded leg of his trousers over long, red claw marks. "Which direction, José?"

The valet checked the sun's position and gestured. "North. Toward Paris."

✣ ✣ ✣

Capitaine Alphonse was entirely receptive to taking on passengers in midvoyage—particularly after José Gregorio presented a fistful of francs. His barge, *La Fleur de Provence*, was named in honor of Madame Mathilde, his good wife. Alphonse adored his wife almost as much as his craft's tiny engine. The latter he kept in shining splendor. The former kept him plump and content with her cooking. As the voyage to Paris took a full week, Wick, Miles, and José Gregorio were in danger of becoming plump themselves.

"Who would have thought . . . " said Wick several days later, as he lay sprawled on his back atop a hold full of ripening melons.

" . . . who would have thought that the *première* barge in all of France, with the *premier* engine of all canal barges of France, could move so slowly?"

"It's probably faster than the horses Alphonse traded the engine for only last year." Miles sighed contentedly next to Wick. "Weren't those *crêpes* Madame whipped up for lunch fabulous?"

"Especially that last one, with Grand Marnier floating all over it," Wick agreed.

José groaned from his reclining position on their other side. "How I'll explain all the wine and all the Grand Marnier to your uncle—"

"What Uncle Eustace doesn't know won't hurt him." Wick chuckled. "Do you suppose he's looking for us yet?"

"We could dash off a telegram to Florence at the next village," Miles suggested, not too enthusiastically.

"We've already discussed keeping clear of the telegraph lines, gentlemen," José observed. "We're taking no chances until after I make my report. That's why we're traveling incognito, as it were, rather than by train."

Miles looked at the valet. "This rest is helping you, José. You're not prison pale anymore. Not even green, like on the airship. And your shoulder seems to have calmed down."

"I wonder what's become of our *Gretchen*," Wick mused. "Sooner or later there'll be farmers swarming all over her—"

"—and the news will spread," José said. "To the local newspapers, then to the national ones. Finally, beyond. It's been three days. Von Klein probably suspects we're somewhere in France. He'll have his people searching for us."

Wick yawned and turned over in the sun. "Can't worry about him now. Time for an afternoon nap. After that I may try a little sketching with the charcoal and paper I picked up in that village this morning. It might not be too late. I'm still only fifteen. Even Albrecht Dürer had to start somewhere."

Miles glanced up the canal. "Another lock coming. Think I'll give Alphonse a hand. He promised to teach me how to fish after we tie up for the night and polish his engine."

✣ ✣ ✣

Paris looked different from the middle of the Seine. Wick—shirt-sleeves rolled above his elbows and buttons opened to his waist past a tanned chest—was steering *La Fleur de Provence* through the barge traffic. He navigated it past the Île de la Cité, a little island in the center of the river. Early afternoon light was reflected by the stained glass of Notre Dame Cathedral as they chugged toward the quay where they would unload their cargo.

Miles stood at the stern in Capitaine Alphonse's second best cap, tending the little engine. José Gregorio was busy admiring the delicate architecture of the bridges spanning the river. Inside the tiny cabin Madame Mathilde was whipping together a farewell feast. Behind Wick, Capitaine Alphonse was puffing at his pipe. He tapped Wick on the shoulder. "*A droite.*" He pointed. "*La bas.*"

Wick spun the wheel to the right and made for the quay as his brother cut the engine. Miles stationed himself by the low hull, ready to leap ashore and fasten the lines. He'd been right about barges all along. Living on one was a great life. If the mysteries of science had not been calling—

"*Nous sommes arrivés!*"

✣ ✣ ✣

They consumed Madame's feast and were smothered in her tearful embrace. At last Wick, Miles, and José Gregorio were back in Paris again, on their own. Wick whistled softly to himself as they walked in the general direction of the Sûreté.

"They truly liked us, Miles. Madame and Capitaine Alphonse. Not for our money or anything else. Just *us*."

Miles was smiling a small, secret smile. "I noticed. They called us *amis*. Friends."

"Good friends," Wick amended.

Miles nodded. "And we've been invited back anytime we're in France. As their guests. For *free*. That's the nicest thing that's happened on this entire trip. And we didn't even work at it."

"On the contrary, gentlemen," José Gregorio interrupted. "You did work at it. Without your adventures, without learning to stretch yourselves—to care about others—you could not have won the hearts of such good people."

"Does that mean we've passed your course, José?" Wick asked. "That we're civilized?"

"Get me inside the Sûreté, and you will have passed with honors," the valet replied.

Wrapped in his thoughts, Miles forged ahead of Wick and José. That's when he noticed an odd, shuttered carriage standing near their destination. He ducked into the closest doorway, then noticed something else. Lurking in the shadows only several doors beyond him was a tall, blond giant of a man—and behind him a caped figure. Miles pressed himself tightly into the space, just as he had in the narrow streets of Nuremberg. He strained to hear the voices.

"Didn't I promise you, Erik?" Pierre Polisson said. "After reading of that balloon appearance in the papers, didn't I say they'd walk directly into our hands?"

"My hands," Erik von Klein muttered.

Miles imagined the villain curling his paws into fists. He squeezed tighter yet into his hideaway.

"My father will forgive me for disappearing in the midst of his search. He will even forgive me for the art missing from his castle walls."

Polisson chuckled. "Timing is all, my friend. We could hardly have ignored the opportunity the graf's castle presented to us. It isn't often empty of servants."

"Yes, perfect timing," Erik agreed. "As it is now!"

"*Now*," Polisson urged, as Wick and José walked past, completely lost in conversation.

Miles opened his mouth to shout a warning, but von Klein was already reaching for his brother. Suddenly, mysterious figures clad in curious, late-medieval dress materialized from the deepening shadows of adjoining buildings. In complete silence they seized the giant just short of his prey. They captured Polisson too.

Oblivious to the little drama, José Gregorio and Wick reached the steps of the Sûreté. Miles sprinted from his hiding place to join them.

"We did it!" he shouted.

He turned to admire Paris, to admire the entire rest of the world that they'd bested. He poked his brother and pointed.

"What?" Wick asked. "*Oh.*"

They watched as two struggling men were shoved into a closed carriage.

"Say, Miles, isn't there something familiar about that carriage? And the cape. . . . It couldn't be—"

"It could and it is." Miles grinned.

José had already opened the bureau's door. Wick's whistle made the valet turn.

"Inside, gentlemen," José Gregorio ordered. "My report is overdue. I'm sure the Dürerbund has little patience with traitors. It will take care of Erik von Klein and Polisson for us."

"And we'll take care of the Dürerbund." Wick smiled with satisfaction.

Miles patted the valet's arm. "Then maybe José can finish giving us our European education. Albrecht's missing works still need to be revealed to the world. And there have to be other courses to pass. Don't you think?"

The valet's mustache twitched.

Author's Note

At the turn of the twentieth century fabulously wealthy Americans decided to spend some of the money they'd accumulated. Andrew Mellon, J. P. Morgan, Hearst, Frick, Widener—all took the Grand Tour of Europe to acquire art by the boatload and ship it home to a young nation they felt was in need of a better cultural image. Eventually, this art became the cornerstone of America's rich museums.

Even Gilded Age robber barons needed guides to this unknown territory. More accustomed to dealing in steel, railroads, mining, and manufacturing, they turned to individuals such as Lord Joseph Duveen—a self-made art dealer with panache—for mentoring. Duveen educated his clients, giving them one-stop courses in the Old Masters of Europe. The works of Renaissance painters such as Albrecht Dürer (1471–1528) suddenly fetched prices that would have shocked their creators.

Albrecht Dürer was the closest thing to a rock star in Renaissance Europe: a handsome, vain, well-traveled, and miraculously gifted artist. Dürer had staying power, too, and went through a periodic revival in Germany. He was the first artist in history to be commemorated by a public monument. The unveiling of his colossal statue in Nuremberg took place in 1840 and was followed by a grandiose four-hundredth birthday celebration in 1871. Plays and music were commissioned and performed. A tidal wave of Dürer kitsch appeared to tempt the masses: metal copies of the statue, stickpins, hairpins, wine glasses, even Albrecht-Dürers-Torte. In 1902 the Dürerbund was established for the purpose of promoting a "healthy" culture. At its peak it had three hundred thousand members and projected an image of the artist which Hitler would later exploit. I have taken great liberties with this organization, but sometimes truth is stranger than fiction.